False Coin, True Coin

HISTORICAL FICTION SET IN THE DAYS OF JOHN BUNYAN

LOIS HOADLEY DICK

JOURNEY FORTH™

Greenville, South Carolina

Library of Congress Cataloging-in-Publication Data:

Dick, Lois Hoadley.
    False coin, true coin / Lois Hoadley Dick.
        p.   cm.
    Summary: After befriending John Bunyan, a prisoner in her
    father's jail, Cissy leaves a life of drudgery for the bustle of
    seventeenth-century London where she endures the horrors of
    the Great Plague and experiences the power of Christ.
        ISBN 0-89084-664-2
        1. Great Britain—History—Charles II, 1660-1685—Juvenile
    fiction. 2. Bunyan, John, 1628-1688—Juvenile fiction. [1. Great
    Britain—History—Charles II, 1660-1685—Fiction. 2. Bunyan,
    John, 1628-1688—Fiction. 3. Christian life—Fiction.] I. Title.
    PZ7.D5466Fal   1993
    [Fic]—dc20   92-39280
                                                                       CIP
                                                                        AC

False Coin, True Coin

Edited by Karen Daniels
Cover by Jamie Miller
Cover Photo Credit: Unusual Films

© 1993 BJU Press
Greenville, South Carolina 29614

Printed in the United States of America

ISBN 0-89084-664-2

20   19   18   17   16   15   14   13   12   11   10   9   8   7

To my editor, Gloria Repp,
who made me rewrite
an adult book
down
to teen-age level,
and who walked with me
every
step
of
the
way

Contents

The Prisoner

The fog crept up from the River Ouse and lay low over the village of Bedford, fifty miles north of London. Cissy Nidd knelt by the small fireplace and coughed. Indeed, she thought, this was the worst fog of the year. Fog always made her cough and wheeze.

Cissy stole a look at her father and two brothers who sat clipping gold and silver coins, slivering off pieces from the edges with sharp knives. After they melted the clippings down in a small iron pan, they dipped coins of base metal into the gold or silver to give them a thin coating.

In all my fifteen years, thought Cissy, I've never seen Pa work so hard at anything. His scurvy thatch of hair, still chestnut brown, fell forward on his handsome face.

"Cissy!" He spoke sharply without looking up. "Where's supper?"

"I'm warming the pie now." She used a folded cloth to lift a hot dish from a ledge built out over the hearth. The savory eel pie, its top crust crispy with lard bubbles, sent up a column of steam as she cut into it.

Her older brother, Harold, glared at her. "Don't make the room any smokier with that fire!" Lank hair, like weeds, straggled down inside the frayed collar of his shirt.

"I'm chilled," Cissy said. "And I got the coughs again."

Her brother Frank, two years younger than Harold, scowled at her too, although he was usually more agreeable. His face was streaked with soot, and dust clung to his curly dark hair. "You're bent on using up our winter coal, ain't you?"

Cissy ignored his ill temper. She knew he was still sore from hauling coal from the river barge up the steps to their small home. They lived over Bedford Jail, halfway across a stone bridge on the river. The jail also served as a tollhouse, and travelers stopped there to pay a fee to the town.

Father's job as jailer and toll collector is a good one, Cissy thought, a good job for 1660. Why did he have to get us all involved in counterfeiting?

She pushed her dark red hair up under the dirty rag around her head, wishing that the fire wouldn't make her face so puffy. Maybe Pa would like her better if she were more handsome. Or if she hadn't been born a girl. Pa had told her often enough that he needed another son for the family business.

Yes, for counterfeiting, she thought. For risking our lives to pass false coin to honest folk. I'll hang at Tyburn someday or have my head stuck on a pole at London Bridge as an example to all good Christians.

Her father tossed down the coin he had been shaving. "Supper!" he roared again. "Are you dreaming over the fire, lazy-bones?" The coin spun and wobbled to a stop.

Cissy sighed and wiped her hands on her skirt. At least she had a home. Thousands of poor folk in the City lived off boiled roots and slept in plank shacks.

"Hot loaves, four for tuppence at the baker's today." She worked up a smile as she stood.

"I seen you slipping Goody Pratt a quarter loaf," Pa said. "You do that again, my girl, and you'll go to bed with an empty belly."

"She's a widow and got no one to fend for her," Cissy murmured. She picked up a cracked pitcher and poured the drink into earthen mugs. "Goody Pratt has been in jail nigh a year now."

"Aye, just deserts for a witch," said Harold.

"She's no witch!" Cissy set the eel pie down in the center of the table. The men pushed their work aside, gouged out slabs of pie, and began to eat.

"Work faster with the lace making, you and Goody," said her father. "Set some of the other female prisoners to watch, and see if they remember what they learn. One of Degrooter's men just rode in from the east coast, and now we've got another sack of false coin to unload in the city. And not near enough bundles of lace to hide it under when you go to London."

Degrooter was the Dutchman who first got Pa into counterfeiting, Cissy remembered. If only he'd stayed in Holland where he belonged.

Harold fingered one of Degrooter's coins. "Look—by wear and tear they lose their design. Can't be sure this Degrooter fellow is dipping them in real gold and silver. All I see is copper. Maybe he's cheating *us!* If only we could have a small stamping press to mold our own designs."

"Illegal," growled Pa. "Even more dangerous than what we're doing now."

"Why does Degrooter want to flood London with bad coin?" asked Frank.

Pa washed down the pie with a long swallow from his mug. "Not satisfied with war between England and Holland, I guess. He wants to make England's money worth nothing. We'd lose the war, no doubt—how can we fight without good money behind us? But little do I care. We'll be safe out of here and into France before then."

Or we'll hang, Cissy thought.

"Couldn't you have boiled up a few turnips from the garden?" Harold complained. "Pie and bread isn't much to go on."

"Didn't have time." Cissy stood up, waiting for them to finish so she could eat the leftovers. "You said to hurry with the lace making."

"Precious little a *girl* can do around here," Pa said. "Except, of course, preening like an ugly duck and planting posies in window boxes." He collected the coins and dropped them into a cloth bag that had a drawstring neck.

Cissy pulled out a bit of flannel cloth from her sleeve and held it over her nose to warm the damp air. She sighed and peered through the window at the fog. Yellow-green murk, layers of it. The River Ouse that ran under the jail seemed to gather up fog and layer it over the village and the entire Midlands of England.

She made a plate for herself of the leftovers and sat in the chimney nook to eat. But before she was half-finished, a sudden, loud thumping at the door downstairs made her jump. Then she heard voices and saw a torch light.

"Visitors! On a night like this!" Pa leaped up from the bench and pulled a heavy curtain over the corner of the room where they kept the coins. "Hurry," he said. "Help me, Frank. Dim the light to one candle, Harold. Quiet . . . shhh, quiet . . . now, Cissy, unbar the door. First ask who 'tis."

Cissy lit a rush taper from the candle and felt her way down the winding wooden steps to the ground floor. "Who is it?" she cried, her mouth to the crack in the door.

"Paul Cobb, Clerk of the Peace! I bring a prisoner for Bedford Jail."

Paul Cobb! Cissy frowned to herself. Paul Cobb, 'most as old as her pa, built like one of the pillars of St. Paul's. Paul Cobb, with his jowly face and a mouth covered with whiskers. He that had tried to kiss her at the hay-making party and told everyone he'd soon ask for her hand.

She hefted the heavy wooden bar and pulled the door open. Beside Master Cobb stood a tall, strong-boned man whose hair and mustache were the color of fresh garden carrots. He was dressed too respectably for a common criminal, Cissy thought.

Then she recognized him. Why, it was the village tinker who lived in Bedford and came and went, preaching around the countryside. The tinker who had married eighteen-year-old Betsy after his wife died and left him with four little ones.

"Well, Cissy, will you not invite us in out of the fog?" Master Cobb asked impatiently.

"Oh, do come in. Pa and I and my brothers took a late supper." Cissy turned her gaze from the red-haired giant and ran nimbly up the steps, the men following.

Pa and the boys rose to greet them. "Evening neighbors. Have a hot drink and some fresh bread?" her father said smoothly. "Daughter, bring clean plates. Terrible night, isn't it, with the fog so early this year?"

"Evening, neighbor Nidd." The prisoner spoke first, and Cissy felt the room fill with a kindliness unknown to her. "Excuse us for arriving at this hour, but I am arrested, as you see, and obliged to spend the night in jail. Only one night, but I'll trouble you to send your girl for my nightcap and a blanket. I give you hearty thanks."

He didn't wait for a reply; he peeled off his dark cloak and stood close to the fire. "Yes, I'll have a bite to eat. Prime fire for a raw night. No doubt I could lie beside it 'til morning. I pledge my word I'll never stir."

"I'm sorry to hear you are detained," said Pa. "Certainly, she shall run across town and fetch your belongings. My dear. . . ." He produced a smile Cissy did not often see. "Go with Master Cobb and take a torch for coming back."

"My pleasure to escort her both ways," Paul Cobb put in quickly.

"No need." Cissy felt fear creep around the back of her neck. She pulled her shawl off a hook. "I know the road like a cat knows the way to the pantry."

Her father smiled again, falsely. "I want no girl of mine out in the fog, mayhap with prowlers lurking behind every hedge." He threw her a warning look and added grimly, "I'm sure you'll respect a father's anguished heart."

No, I'll not have him, Cissy answered silently. You can't make me.

"If you will just sign here that I delivered the prisoner, I think this affair about his preaching will straighten itself out in a short time." Master Cobb held out a paper, and Pa scratched his name on the bottom. "Please come, Mistress Nidd."

Cissy abruptly hooked her shawl back up on the nail and sat down hard on a four-legged stool. She picked up her work pillow and placed it on her lap. *Clack-clack,* the bobbins tapped out her determination. She and Paul Cobb out together in the fog? Never! With straight pins she pricked out a scroll and leaf pattern.

"I do thank you, Master Cobb, but I must finish my lace. I'm sure Frank can loan an extra nightcap to the prisoner, and, of course, we have a blanket to spare. I'm afeared to go outdoors because of my coughs worsening." She covered her mouth with the flannel rag and forced a choking spell.

She waited a little fearfully for Paul Cobb to speak. He was an important man in Bedford, and perhaps she shouldn't have offended him. But *marry* that fellow? No, no, and no again.

Obviously swallowing his disappointment, Master Cobb said, "As you will, Mistress Nidd. I look forward to walking you home from Divine Service next Sunday."

The men bowed to each other, and the Clerk of the Peace took his leave. Cissy waited until she heard the oak door close, then ran down to set up the bar. As she reached for it, an arm encircled her waist and Paul Cobb's beefy face searched for hers. He'd tricked her!

"Come, be a little friendly."

Silently she struggled against him, writhing out of his grasp. Her foot felt for the bottom step.

"You haven't been in Divine Service these three Sundays, Cissy," he said angrily. "If you miss the fourth, it will be my unhappy duty to issue you a formal warning, according to the Declaration of Parliament."

He lurched out of the door, slamming it behind him. Cissy barred it with shaky hands and ran upstairs. She crouched on her stool and reached again for the lace and bobbins. Now I like him less than ever, she thought.

The four men talked amiably, sitting around the wooden table, and Cissy listened. How ridiculous to arrest a man for preaching as Master Bunyan does, she thought. How good of him to promise to stay arrested and not run off! She smiled a little to herself.

The prisoner turned to include Cissy in the conversation. ". . . and there were, gentlemen, two hundred of us, gathered to worship God. In comes the constable and his soldiers. 'Seize the weapons!' they cry. 'Where are the weapons?' "

Bunyan broke off to laugh heartily. "In spite of myself, I had to laugh. I'd even known they would come to arrest me that night, being forewarned."

Frank leaned forward, his arms crossed on the table. "Where *were* the weapons, Master Bunyan?"

Master Bunyan gazed at him steadily, then looked at the other two men. "You really don't understand, do you? Dissenters don't want to overthrow the government. Can't you understand that there are Christians who want something more than reading a prayer from the Prayer Book?"

Cissy stared at him as he went on. "Many people fall asleep in the churches during long-winded sermons and the play acting of ritual. But the sermons are bare of God's Word! I was only preaching in the barn. There were no weapons!"

A scowl crossed Pa's handsome face, and he stretched. "The law says that no more than four may gather. When you have a mob of people, you'll have rebellions, uprisings, and who knows what. Secret meetings are forbidden. Ain't too unreasonable to ask people to attend Divine Service once a month or so. I'm always there, being a jailer and a person of position in Bedford."

"Once a month." Master Bunyan grinned.

Aye, like false coin Pa is, thought Cissy. Dipped a little bit into religion, but bad enough underneath.

"Every single month," Harold burst out, "we're obliged to listen to that boring twit, for he has naught to say. Else we'd be first given a warning, then arrested, then shipped to the Barbados as slaves! All for the sake of churchgoing."

"Shut your mouth; you're talking treason," Pa growled under his breath. To Master Bunyan he said, "You're welcome to stay by the fire tonight. The town council must bring a formal written accusation against you. If you promise to preach no more, all may go well."

This man will never promise to stop preaching, Cissy thought, remembering that he'd once preached to three thousand people in London. Another time, she'd heard, he stood on the edge of a cliff and preached to over a thousand folk who sat on the grass.

"I run a respectable jail," Pa was saying. "We're all law-abiding, God-fearing Christians in this place. We get our living plus ten pounds a year. We've got the vegetable garden out back. Cissy, here, makes elegant lace to sell in London town. I put every shilling away for her dowry," he added piously.

Liar, thought Cissy. Every half-penny goes into Pa's pocket and cries out, it is pinched so tightly.

Master Bunyan stood up at the mention of lace, crossing the room to stand by her and watch. "Allow me?" He took up a handful of bobbins, and under his skillful fingers, the lacy design formed. "The thread is brittle and ready to snap," he observed. "Bobbin lace is best done in a damp cellar."

"Down in the jail!" Frank laughed.

Cissy scanned the bit of lace Master Bunyan had made. "How quick you are! Much faster than I am! Amazed I am, for fair! How could you know to make lace?"

"A tinker does much more than mend pots and pans and sell ladies' trifles. When I was five, I attended lace school in Mistress Elwin's cottage with over thirty other young ones. We stuck ten pins a minute, six hundred an hour. We marked out the pattern with our baby hands. If we grew slothful—whack!—her cane switched our bare necks.''

"This lace is for a lady's parasol," Cissy explained.

"All my children except Blind Mary work at lace."

Pa lifted the lace Master Bunyan had made and held it close to the candle flame. "Excellent. You have not lost your skill, for being a gypsy tinker. There is great demand for such lace just now. Could you teach prisoners to make bobbin lace?"

"Prisoners are no different than we are. Am I not a prisoner?" Master Bunyan smiled, sitting down on the side of the hearth. "If they are nimble with their fingers, they could surely learn to make lace."

Pa switched to another subject. "You look old enough to have served in Oliver Cromwell's army. You stand tall and stiff like a soldier."

"Aye, neighbor, I went to war when I was sixteen. There was no king in the land, and no one else offered leadership. Our men were a mixture of Presbyterians and Independents. We sang hymns and prayed together, all of one faith. We had freedom of conscience, then. Why could it not be like that always?"

"Your kind be sour Puritans."

"And the sour milk best flavors the cake."

Pa laughed. "Some things we'll never agree on, Neighbor Bunyan, though we talk 'til the candle melts down. I'm loyal to the reigning master, whoever he is at the time. My job depends 'pon it. I'm loyal to the Established Church and the laws of the land. As are my boys."

Pa squinted at Cissy's brothers, and they both chorused, "The King, God bless 'im!"

"I'd as soon turn Turk," Harold volunteered, "as be a Dissenter."

"To Charles II." Pa lifted his mug. "Ah, you won't drink to it, neighbor?"

"Dissenters don't drink or swear oaths," answered Master Bunyan. "As for earthly kings, they are like the men we see on the river—they look one way and row the other. There are a few of us who think the common people should have a voice in the governing of this nation. What is any nation, but for its common people? The girl—your daughter—how thinks she on such matters?"

Pa shrugged, ignoring Cissy. "She's an empty head."

Cissy flushed and pressed her lips together. The prisoner was a strange one, treating her like one of the family, asking her opinion, expecting her to have an opinion.

"I believe all people of the realm are equal before God," Master Bunyan went on. "I believe conversion to Christ lifts any poor laborer into the rank of earl as far as God is concerned. Why, in God's sight, your daughter here is on the same level as a queen."

Cissy looked up, astonished. How dared he talk like that! She sat a little taller.

"This is all most interesting to me," said Pa. "I certainly believe in looking at both sides of a coin."

Frank snickered at the pun.

"I like a fearless man who speaks out," Pa continued. "Did you see the execution of Charles I?"

"I did."

"I was laid up with a fever."

" 'Twas January 31, 1649, a bitterly cold day. Thousands of people jammed the square outside Whitehall Palace."

I was but four years old, Cissy thought.

"I recollect how the wooden platform swayed in the wind and the king knelt at the block," said Master Bunyan. "In a moment it was over. A groan burst from the crowd. They thought it a crime against God to execute even a wicked king. But I felt in my own soul that rule by divine right was over. And a good thing, too, for our rulers have been as wicked and base as any heathen. They lived in ease while their subjects starved."

Master Bunyan leaned forward to gaze earnestly at Pa while the candle flame stretched high between them and swayed at his breath. "We Dissenters left the Church. We weren't able to purify it and turn it back to God's Word as the authority. Folks say I can't understand Scripture because I do not know the Hebrew, Greek, or Latin. But I have known temptations which drove me to God. I have known His power that breaks the power of sin. I have the Holy Spirit to explain His Word. What do I lack?"

Cissy watched for her father's reaction, but he only said, "It will go hard for the Dissenters, now that Parliament has dismissed itself."

Master Bunyan fell silent for a moment. Then he said, "I'm keeping you from bed, and I'm burning your candle." Frank and Harold nodded good night, and Pa stood up. "Cissy, fetch a blanket for Master Bunyan; then do you get abed. Neighbor, I'll bid you good night as we are early risers."

After the brothers left the room, Master Bunyan said to Pa, "Stay a minute!"

Cissy turned at the sound of his voice. The prisoner was studying her. "We be but three in the room, so I can preach. I'm not breaking the law. I feel obliged to say this much in benediction, good people."

His nod included Pa, but he spoke directly to Cissy. "The Lord says through His prophet Jeremiah, *Yea, I have loved thee with an everlasting love.*"

The Black Pot

The weeks piled up almost as fast as the lace the prisoners had learned to make. The months passed quickly too, and the pile of counterfeit coin in the closet grew higher. Spring came to Bedford town. Cissy found the first violets, dug up a plant, and brought it home for her window box.

"Last one up is an April fool!" cried Frank, scrambling out of bed the first morning in April.

"When do we leave for London?" Cissy didn't feel like April fooling. It seemed that she could still hear the sad tolling of the bass church bell for the death of Master Bunyan's baby, even though half a year had gone by. When Mistress Bunyan had heard of her husband's arrest, her pains began. For eight days she was unable to deliver, and then the baby had been born dead.

Cissy leaned her arms on the windowsill, her nose in the violets. "All he had to do was promise not to preach," she said aloud, "and he would not."

"Huh?" Frank searched in the cupboard for bread. "What are you rambling about? You should be excited that we are going to see King Charles II crowned."

"I'll be glad to get away from here; that's the truth. Nothing happens in Bedford but sadness. How hard it must be for Mistress Bunyan, with him still in jail and four little ones to care for!"

"Paul Cobb visited him Monday last," replied Frank, "to warn him again that he could be banished from the country—or hung. His house and goods would be taken and his family turned out on the street. And still the fool said, 'Were I out of prison today, I would preach the gospel tomorrow.' "

"Is not such harshness strange for a country calling itself Christian?" Cissy filled a tin cup with water from a big jug by the door and gave her violets a drink. "I heard in town that Master Bunyan offered to show all his sermon notes to the judges so they could see if he preached against the king. They weren't interested. Still, it puzzles me that he calls his secret meetings 'the church.' Should not a church have a beautiful sanctuary and a fine organ?"

"He's a stubborn man, a nobody who wants to be a somebody. He could make a good living tinkering if only he stopped playing preacher." Frank ended the conversation by going downstairs to take the prisoners water.

Cissy began spring cleaning, knocking down cobwebs from the ceiling with a broom, and reaching into every crack and corner. She raised such dust that she brought on a coughing spell.

She cleaned one room a day, washing down the wooden floor and then hanging all the woolen clothes out in the sun to air. As she worked, she thought of Master Bunyan, in Bedford Jail these many months, waiting for his trial. She wondered what his future would be.

Early one morning, she and Frank started out for London even before the skylark sang. The counterfeit coin was hidden in a sack under bundles of bobbin lace. Cissy's long red hair was pinned up so that it wasn't any longer than Frank's, and then covered by a man's hat. She wore an old suit of Frank's. Disguised as a boy, no one would recognize her as a jailer's daughter.

Frank had coaxed a little beard to grow and wore his cap low over his forehead and a new suit no one in Bedford had ever seen.

"Fifty miles to London," he said gaily. "We'll stay in Luton tonight with one of Pa's contacts."

Cissy sat her horse as well as any man. They rode down Watling Street and out onto the country road going south. I'm into wrongdoing, she thought miserably, and well enough I know it. Should I refuse, Pa would marry me straightway to Paul Cobb. Aloud she said, "Frank, I'm feared. . . ."

"Pray, don't begin that now," her brother interrupted. "Think of the sport we'll have and the extra money to spend."

Cissy drew in deep breaths of air sweet with the scent of hawthorn. Past meadows and waterfalls they rode, past marshes and willow trees.

They left Bradford County and rode down through Hertford County. The coronation was to be held that very week. Cissy wondered what souvenirs she could buy. Maybe hair ribbons, or an apron with a flower on the pocket to embroider, or a packet of seeds for her window box. Peddlers from all over England would be there.

After a few hours, other travelers joined them. They reached Luton, then rode single file over a long path through a woodsy dell to stay with Master Greaves. The second night they stayed over in Hertford. Leaving St. Albans the third day, they approached the city walls of London at last.

"Look, Frank!" Cissy pointed at the little flower girls who ran along the road, offering stalks of lavender and sunflowers.

"Posies, posies, fresh from the meadow!" they cried. Nearby, a farmer's wife rode astride an old mare, burdened down with noisy piglets to sell. The woman laughed and bought a posy.

"Now you'll see people—people—people—like wheat in a barrel." Frank gestured toward the human bodies pushing, shouting, laughing, pressing toward the gates. "Six hundred thousand inside one square mile! Isn't that an amazement? We're here Cissy! We're in London!"

I could still turn back, Cissy thought. I could say no to the unlawful business I shall do this week. But Pa would turn me out. Where would I go? Who would take care of me?

She looked around herself and saw a thousand chimney tops belching black, sooty smoke. Grimy warehouses and soap factories rose on either side. Slummy, winding alleys turned off the main road. Coaches and carts rattled over the cobbled streets.

"Ride straight down Aldersgate Street," said Frank. "Turn left onto Cheapside; it's the shortest way."

Cissy spied the Gold Rose Tavern. "Can we breakfast here?"

"All right. Tie your horse to the post over there. They have the best clangers here I ever did eat. Here, let me carry in the sacks of lace."

He ordered the suet pudding of chopped beef, liver, and potatoes. Cissy ate hungrily.

"You could learn to make us a clanger like this," Frank said.

"Sounds like a church bell." Cissy started to smile, then remembered Master Bunyan's baby and the church bell. And will it toll for me, she wondered, if I be caught at this business?

Back out in the excitement of the streets, she mounted her horse, and they continued down Aldersgate Street. She could see the spires of St. Paul's Cathedral, high on Ludgate Hill. She'd heard it was the biggest church in the world.

"Cowcumbers! Cowcumbers!" howled a street vender. "Growed by the watermill! Cow-w-w-w-cumbers!"

"I love to hear them," she said. "Frank, why are we turning?"

"We must go through Cheapside. But don't be fooled by its name. This is one of the most expensive sections of London. See the mansions? There's Goldsmith's Row, with twelve of the most magnificent homes in all of England. The king will ride past here on his way to claim the throne."

"I wish I lived here. I love these shops!" Cissy called ahead to her brother. "Where's the river? I've heard so much about it. And I'd love to look inside a really big church—they have such beautiful altars."

"Dismount and walk now!" bellowed Frank over the noise of passing carriages and wheelbarrows. "Keep straight, then turn right toward Fish Hill. That takes us down to London Bridge.'' A hackney carriage barely squeezed by them, scraping the door of a house. Sedan chairs swung past with frowning men inside.

Cissy edged through the narrow, cobbled street. Most houses were built of logs with red brick between each layer, a pretty patterned sight. But the slimy streets were crowded with cats and dogs. ''Oh!'' Cissy cried out and ducked back as a maid emptied a bucket of water from an upstairs window.

From the top of Fish Hill Road, she saw the Thames River winding in from the ocean like a brown sea serpent. Tall masts of ships from all nations rose from the dirty water. ''There's London Bridge!''

''Four hundred years old,'' said Frank. ''Still standing.''

Cissy, looking down the hill, thought the bridge looked like another one of London's narrow and congested streets taken up and hung across the Thames on solid stone arms. The poorly built houses were kept from toppling into the river by iron tie bars reaching from rooftop to rooftop.

''Cresses, fresh green cresses, sir,'' cried a swarm of little watercress girls running up the hill toward Cissy, their hands red and chapped from working in cold water. ''Take some home to your lady.'' Cissy shook her head, and they scattered.

Farther down the hill, Cissy stopped to stare at a puppet show put on by a grinning fellow behind a cardboard stage. ''Look, Frank. Can we watch?''

''No, the Metcalfs are waiting for us. Get along down to the Bridge, do.''

''Good day, pie man! A sunny morrow to you, muffin man! Oh, Frank, there must be thousands of people here making a living on the river and the banks. Oh, I want to see everything! Here's a boat being hammered together! Frank, don't hurry me! Here's a little rhubarb girl—oh, what a pie I could make of that!''

''Get along, I say!''

Cissy led her horse onto Lower Thames Street, past damp caves built into the banks of the river. She smelled tar and new rope. Under London Bridge the water ran in cataracts, and she counted nineteen arching piers. Spray flew into her eyes as they drew closer.

"High tide," Frank noted. "Hurry along, Cis. The Metcalf's inn, The Black Pot, is partway across the Bridge, next to the button maker's shop."

A few fashionable houses dressed up London Bridge, but most were shops of sail makers, shoemakers, and merchants. Homeless beggars curled up in doorways.

They passed an open door, and Cissy saw a sawdust-covered floor and neat wooden tables and benches. She smelled onions cooking.

The owner spied them for travelers. "Coffee, my good young sirs? A nice dish of cabbage with a slice of sausage pudding? Come, try the new "China Drink"—my good wife calls it *tea*."

Cissy looked in longingly and her mouth watered, but Frank shook his head. "Much obliged, but we dine at The Black Pot."

A few yards further, he stopped in front of a building where a large black kettle hung overhead. Cissy tied her horse to a hitching post and stepped through the door into a dim room. Frank followed, carrying the three saddlebags.

Peg Metcalf bustled out from the kitchen and hugged them both. Her gaudy red and purple dress was partly covered with a white apron, and she wore a crisp lace cap.

"God save the king! Lord bless us all!" she shrieked. "We're promised a beautiful day for tomorrow, lads!" She winked at Cissy. "I espied you coming as I looked out the door, and I have an eye to your happiness, lads. I've laid a cloth and served up a beef stew in two little pots along with hot breads fresh made. And pigs' feet in jelly!"

"Right glad we are to be here." Frank grinned. "How have you been, Auntie Peg?"

"I'll Auntie Peg you! I'm just plain Peg to all, my young blade!" Her face, blowzy-red from the oven heat, crinkled into laugh lines.

"I'm fair glad to see you," Cissy said. They took chairs in a quiet corner of the room and began to eat. She admired the stew served in miniature black pots that were replicas of the great pot hanging outside.

Frank spooned meat and potatoes into his mouth. "Where's Trig?"

"Master Metcalf is sleeping like an innocent!" Peg guffawed loudly, then put her head close to theirs. "Had business on the river late last night. I'm sure you understand. He'll be up shortly."

She handed Cissy a dish of butter. "Child, you're a woman grown, I vow! I saw you as a wee one once, but you'll not remember. When are you going to come and stay with old Peg? I'll dress you up fine to meet some of the dandies that take their supper here."

"Not Cissy–she's just a country wench," said Frank.

Cissy felt her face grow hot, and she chewed down hard on her bread.

"Never learned to smirk behind a fan, either," Frank added.

"Nay, you are a villain!" Peg retorted. "Cissy is just all at sixes and sevens right now; 'tis her age. She ain't blossomed yet. Plain she is, yes, but she's a pretty underneath. If she were tricked out in a flowered gown with a petticoat, Cissy'd turn some gallant's head. She's just shy."

"She'll marry well," Frank said. "Pa will see to that."

"Frank only comes to the city to look over the girls," Cissy retorted. "Sweet little Nellie back home would love to hear some tittle-tattle of Frank in the city."

"Now stop, children. Peace. I'll have no more teasing. Cissy, I am serious about you coming to stay here. There's something unwholesome about a girl living in that jail of yours. How's your Pa?"

"He's well." Cissy attacked a large slab of apple pudding that had spice sauce running down its sides.

Peg gave a wink that creased her plump face in half. "His talents is wasted in a jail house, ain't they?" She refilled Cissy's coffee mug and changed the subject. "Have you shopping to do? Ah, I am sure of it. You two young ones shop on the Bridge awhile, and I'll dispose of the *lace*." Her voice underlined the word.

"Three bags full." Frank kicked the saddlebags he'd stowed under the table. He lowered his voice. "Will we ever meet the man called Degrooter, Peg?"

"Hush! That's not a name to say lightly and not a name to mention at all in daylight. I would not want it known he comes here."

Cissy shivered, though she wasn't at all cold. She certainly did not want to meet the man her father worked for. Why, he could blackmail them all if they ever quit passing false coin. She pictured him as large and evil looking, with hard eyes and a quick sword.

She and Frank spent the afternoon on the Bridge and the waterfront. "Look, Frank," Cissy said. She stared into the window of an old clothes shop, then ran inside. "Here's a bonnet for a penny!" She handed over a penny and came out with the hat. Made of faded pink linen, the bonnet was loaded with artificial morning-glories on top.

"Well, you *are* an apple head!" was Frank's reaction. "Wait 'til Pa sees that!"

But Cissy wasn't listening. She saw a man making ladies' slippers from soft leather imported from Spain. "Oh, Frank, ask him to fit me for a pair—do!"

"Turn away!" Frank snapped. "Do you forget you're in disguise—dressed as a man?"

Cissy sniffed and turned away from the slippers. She felt foolish carrying a lady's pink bonnet, but no one in the crowd seemed to notice.

At Billingsgate, by the left entrance of London Bridge, they watched fishermen unload their catch. Cissy climbed out onto the quay, where a dozen boats were tied up for the day. Men threw out nets of squirming, shining fish.

"Tuppence a tail!" screamed the fishwives, all fat women with baskets on their arms. "Or four tails for a penny for the wee ones! Fish for yer pot. Fresh and saucy!"

Cissy's feet hurt from walking in men's boots, and she was glad to return to The Black Pot and nap in a corner of Peg's bedroom.

In the lull before the eight o'clock diners arrived, Trig Metcalf appeared. Yawning, he walked to the back table where Cissy and Frank sat.

He held out his hand to them both. "Well, I declare. Frank Nidd and Cissy." Cissy remembered to clasp hands, as Frank did.

Trig was as trim as his wife was large. His eyes were small, his nose a mere garnish on his face. In his brown shirt and breeches and hose, he reminded Cissy of a dried herring. Even his voice was dry.

Peg served up platters of meat and vegetables. "This is grand," Cissy said happily. "More food than ever I've had at one time. The mutton is fair tasty, Peg."

When they began the dessert of walnut cake, Trig found his tongue. "Tell your Pa the lace is just fine. We'll have no trouble selling it. And the other—the trimmings that accompany the lace—shall I call them lace clippings? Ha-ha! I see Wicket takes his fair share, but it's all right. Degrooter is a generous man. Just don't clip the *lace* too small."

"Speak softer, do!" Peg kept glancing at the doorway. "Even the pot has ears."

"We daren't have a real stamping press to turn out thousands of coins a day like they do at the Mint." Frank helped himself to extra cake. "Pa makes coins one at a time, then stamps them with the designs you send him. 'Tis very slow work."

Trig gave his knife a final lick. "Tell him to be most cautious. Tell him Thomas Simon, the engraver to the king, has cut a special seal for a solid gold Coronation Medal."

"Can we see one?" Cissy asked.

"Better than that." Trig leaned closer to the table. "I have a copy of it, and you can take it to your Pa, and he can work quickly and make some counterfeit ones and send them back to me. This is a coin made in honor of the new king, and we will never see its like again. Degrooter will pay well for this favor."

Cissy twisted uneasily on the hard bench. Nobody knew that she, too, helped herself to a bit of the profit. Buried under the lilac bush at home was a small metal box with a handful of coins she called her "dowry money." Supposing she did wed someday, Pa wasn't likely to give her anything.

Still, it was stolen money. Mayhap she would donate some of it to the church in Bedford to smother her conscience. She could slip it, unseen, into the plate so people wouldn't wonder that she had so much.

She licked her fingers after eating some sticky date sweets. "This man Degrooter hates England, doesn't he?"

"Aye, only natural; he's a Dutchman. Do you know what the new king has already done to all of us honest merchants? Closed the Bank of England while he cut the worth of all English money in half. Many of us hope he's cut right off his throne."

"You never saw milady's beautiful home in the Midlands, Cissy," said Peg. "The lady I cooked for had servants, horses, vacations. Fine linen tablecloths! All lost now, because of King Charles II. And here we live, in this outlandish black pot arrangement. Me, with my hands into the dirty water and greasy dishes all day long!"

They fell silent until Cissy said, "Peg, you have a lovely eating place. All the gentlemen crossing the Bridge to Southwark stop here. And your idea to serve up the stew in little black pots is delightful."

" 'Twasn't my idea. A tinker who once lived on the Bridge advised me. John Bunyan was a clever man."

"John Bunyan! The giant with red hair who preaches in secret meetings?" Frank stirred his coffee hard. "A Dissenter?"

"The same. Though he preached openly then."

"Why, he is in our jail!" Cissy exclaimed. And wouldn't she die from shame were Master Bunyan to know where *she* was, and why.

"Now that's a pity." Peg brushed crumbs from the table with a flat knife and a tray. "I attend church, naturally, and what a time I have staying awake. But I heard Master Bunyan preach in London once, and he went on and on, nigh two hours. Do you know—I never shut an eye!"

"I figure my ledger book while sitting in church," Trig said.

"My mind works out a new lace pattern," Cissy admitted.

"My mind's on Nellie," Frank said. "I can just see her out of the corner of my eye. One of these Sundays I'll make bold to speak to her."

Two gentlemen with their ladies strolled through the door. "Are we early, Mistress Metcalf?"

Peg jumped up to welcome them. Ushering them to chairs by the window, she went back into the kitchen for a pitcher of hot drink. Supper time for guests had begun at The Black Pot.

Cissy could hardly keep awake. She wanted to watch the fine people on their way to the theaters in Southwark, but she began to yawn. Finally, she said good night and retired. Peg had curtained off a corner of the bedroom for her and had laid clean nightclothes on the trundle bed.

She knelt on the bed and looked out of the little lead-paned window, listening to the rush of the river just under the inn. There was a full moon. She could see the Thames, inky violet, with masts and chimneys like quill pen stabbings done in black. A square-rigged ship, sails furled for the night, rocked at anchor. Boats like small sardines skimmed past on mysterious business.

We be counterfeiters and smugglers and traitors to the Crown, Cissy thought sadly. Liars, cheats, thieves. Betrayers of our country, making it weak for war with Holland.

She pushed open one of the little windows and let the cool night air blow across her face. "And I be a great sinner, almost as bad as Wicket Nidd, my own father."

"Wicket Nidd—Wicked Nidd." Drowsily she played with the sound of the name.

"And Master Bunyan be a true man of God."

With these confused and troubled thoughts, she lay down, pulled the quilt over her head, and fell asleep.

Coronation Day

April 23, 1661, Coronation Day. The great noisy splashing water wheel of London Bridge had awakened Cissy early. She looked out of the window just in time to see the drawbridge part in two and rise to let a ship pass. The gears ground and the drawbridge lowered itself with a thud that shook the house.

A most fair day, she thought, and I shall see a king crowned! Ostrich feathers of smoke floated down from the neighboring chimney tops and partly blurred her view.

"New clothes for the young gentlemen!" Peg entered the room, holding up two suits, shirts, and plumed hats. "This way you and Frank can shop in the best of shops and spend that false coin without being suspected."

Cissy pulled on dark blue breeches and a silk shirt and slung a man's purse over one arm. The dark cloak lined in red would make her look like a brother to Frank.

"Braid your hair and pin it up under this cap," Peg said. "Pull some loose hair down over your ears. There, the cap covers your head down to your eyebrows. Too bad I can't trim those long curly eyelashes; mayhap they will give away your secret."

Cissy ate heartily at breakfast and finished with a hot drink. She could hear the river traffic growing louder, and outside, a hurdy-gurdy woman was whacking out a shrill tune on her instrument.

"Trig and I will bide here," said Peg. "The Black Pot will do a grand bit of business today, what with serving meals and giving change in our new coin." She winked at Cissy. "Next time, you stay a little longer with old Peg. She'll dress you up like a fine lady, and we'll go to the theater in Southwark."

"Cissy's to wed Paul Cobb, Pa says." Frank smoothed his shoulder-length hair and cocked his hat at an angle. "Hurry on, Cis."

"Don't ever say that again!" Cissy flared at him. "You be a bubble-headed dunce to think I'd wed with that man. I'll see me a spinster or in my grave afore that!"

"Tush, tush, children." Peg soothed them both. "Have you each two purses? Put one on display under your right arm, the other hidden on the left. Pay out from the right-side purse with the false coin. Put the true coin into the hidden purse. Now then, you look fine; a pair of brave young gentlemen, off to see the Coronation."

"Much we'll see of it." Cissy tossed the cloak over her shoulder. "Thousands of other people will be ahead of us, and the best seats on the scaffolding are given to the rich."

"Never mind the scaffolding," Peg told them. "Creep around the crowd, closer and closer to Westminster Abbey. Say, 'Pray let us through; we are part of the procession.' "

Trig came into the dining room carrying two fancy walking canes for them. "You be here to pass the coin, not to see the Coronation," he grumbled.

Peg shooed Cissy and Frank outside. "You have yourselves a good time. Buy, buy! Pay in false and bring back true! God save the king!"

Even at seven o'clock in the morning London Bridge was alive with people in holiday clothes, and excitement spread from one person to another.

The Thames was at low tide, and Cissy saw homeless children and crippled old folks poking in the muck for nails or coins or pieces of coal to sell. "They're called *mudlarks*," Frank explained. "They live in the big sewers and make as much as a half penny a day. They find bones and rope and spoons and things folk drop what got washed down the sewer."

"Isn't it dangerous?"

"Of course. Aren't you glad you live in a better place?"

Do I live in a better place? Cissy asked herself. Am I glad? She didn't have an answer.

"Move along now; we have a long walk." Frank guided her off the Bridge and toward St. Paul's in the distance. They passed the Temple Bar where lawyers worked. The streets were clogged with people, off to see the Coronation. Cissy felt she was drowning in a sea of people. Twice Frank had to seize her arm and pull her along. "We will never get to see a thing," she mourned aloud. "Why don't we stay on the outskirts of the crowd and pass coin only inside the shops?"

"We are going to see the king," Frank replied stubbornly. "I have a plan."

They reached a street corner and stopped under a shop awning. "Look here." Frank unrolled two long silver ribbons from his pocket. He pinned one across Cissy's chest from her left shoulder down to her right hip. The ribbon was decorated with pearl buttons spelling out the initials CS—Charles Stuart, the king's legal name.

Frank pinned the other ribbon on himself. "Now we're venders. And venders can go anywhere."

Cissy pointed out sellers of cheap bracelets and ear bobs, toys and candy. "Shall we deal in goodies?"

"No. Programs, that's what we want. I say, sir!" Frank hailed two old men. "How much will you take for your trays with the scrolls on them? We mean to play at peddling today for a lark."

Unbelief spread over one man's face. "It's me livin'; I can't part with me livin'."

"I'm going to pay you more than you'd earn, my good man, and you can go off and enjoy the Coronation without any bother."

Both old men hung back. "I'd make near five shilling today," the taller one said.

"I'll give you ten shillings each."

"The tray is handmade by me brother what is a carpenter on the quay," the tall one added.

Frank pulled open his purse of false coin. "A pound for each of you, only because I have a rich uncle in Parliament."

The men slipped the leather straps off their shoulders and laid down the trays. "It's our bounden dooty to go off and pick pockets in the crowd so's the rich won't be heavy laden," said the first.

"Thank you kindly, young gentlemen, and may you have a good day," ventured the second.

Cissy's heart felt heavy. Should the old men be caught with false coin, it would go hard with them, and all because of us, she thought.

"Carry your tray and follow me." Frank headed for the scaffolding, where nobles and wealthy families had been waiting for hours to see the king.

Cissy looked up at the balconies and windows jammed with people. Along the procession way, a blue carpet stretched from the Abbey to Westminster Hall, where the king would banquet with the House of Lords. Cissy knew the ceremony by heart from hearing the talk of Bedford townfolk.

First, the Knights of the Bath would bear the heavy platters of food to the king's table, escorted by servants. Then the King's Champion, a knight in armor, would ride in on a splendid steed to throw down the gauntlet, challenging any man to step forward and say why Charles II should not be king.

"Why are we standing here so long? My back aches." Cissy leaned against the bottom of the scaffolding and waited for Frank to tell her what to do.

Finally, when the first sound of trumpets could be heard in the distance, Frank jolted her alert. "Now, follow me," he said. "Do what I do! We are going to the top of that scaffolding."

He stepped out from under the stand and began to push his way through the mob, shouting, "Make way! Free programs for the ladies!"

A few women heard the call and stretched out their hands. Others heard and made way for the venders. "Let us pass!" shouted Frank. "Free programs, compliments of His Majesty!"

Cissy shouldered her way through the people, following Frank. In a short time they were on the scaffolding. Slowly they climbed up the narrow aisle, distributing the scrolls as they went. The sound of trumpets grew louder. Cissy reached the very top row and eagerly looked down upon the scene.

All the buildings were hung with rich tapestries. The ladies showered posies onto the street. "Oh, isn't it splendid?" Cissy laughed aloud. "The finest parade I ever did see! The coaches look like bulging pumpkins from our garden! See the lace round the coachmen's necks? That's handmade bobbin lace, or I'm not Cissy Nidd!"

The flashing, gem-studded armor and helmets so dazzled her eyes that she had to blink. Next in the procession marched the Duke of York's Horse Guards and Knights of the Bath, all in cloth of gold and emeralds.

At last Cissy saw the king. He was robed in ermine, riding on a white horse under a canopy of silver cloth carried by six barons. His wavy black hair fell below his shoulders, and his full lips smiled at the crowd. He rode straight into Westminster Abbey. There, a brief service was held that those outside could not see. Cissy heard the anthem sung by combined choirs of all the churches in London. Most likely in heaven they hear singing like this every single blessed day, she thought in awe.

Suddenly all the bells of all the churches in London struck the noon hour. Though Cissy could not see it, she knew the crown of England now rested on the head of their lawful king. When he reappeared on the street with the Archbishop of Canterbury beside him, a shout went up from ten thousand throats. "God save the king!"

Cissy felt the scaffold tremble and sway. Now the bells pealed like divine thunder, and the sound clanged in her head until she felt giddy and leaned against Frank lest she faint. "Long live his majesty, King Charles II!" She wanted to join in the cry, but she could only whisper.

Would England be happy now after all her trouble? Would there be a better life for all, as her father predicted? And what of Cissy Nidd?

She stood unmoving on the scaffolding as the frock-coated gentlemen and their ladies began to depart, going off to dine or ride in the country as was the custom. The golden music of the bells died away. Still Cissy didn't move.

"Well, now!" Frank shook her arm. "You have seen a king. Throw that ribbon away and drop the tray. We're off to buy with false and get change in true. While you were gawking like a stage-silly, I have cut two purses with my sharp little scissors; and well paid we'll be, for they were rare gentlemen."

Cissy stared at him in alarm. "Frank! You, a cutpurse? They didn't see you, did they?"

"Never even missed the purses, so set were they on bellowing and bawling greetings down to the king. The purses are chock-full of large gold and silver pieces. I tied them under my arm next to my shirt."

Climbing slowly down the scaffolding, Cissy remembered something. "I didn't buy any souvenirs to remind me of this day. Though I vow I'll never—no I'll never—forget the parade and the bells. I fancy a silver thimble or a new pattern book and a bolt of cloth."

"Fine noise it was," Frank agreed. "Buy whatever you like. Mayhap you'll see combs and such from a far country."

Further down the street, people crowded around a farmer who was flourishing a whip and selling books that were piled on his cart next to bales of hay. "I can read fair well," Cissy said wistfully. "Frank, don't you ever wonder what's in the big books in the stalls near St. Paul's? The books rich people have. Can we walk over to Bookseller's Row sometime?"

"Not today." Frank stopped, took a few steps, stopped again and shaded his eyes with one hand.

"What is it?"

"Look yonder! Don't you recognize him?"

They walked closer to the farmer selling books, and Cissy looked up at him closely. His hair was covered with a rough cap and he wore hobnail boots, but there was no hiding the orangy moustache nor the deep preacher's voice.

"Master Bunyan!" Cissy exclaimed, shocked. "He's here, preaching in London! And selling Bibles!"

"Don't let him see us like this!" Frank grasped her hand, but it was too late. Master Bunyan pointed at them with his whip. "Ah, friends from back home! Now I know you'll want a Geneva Bible, only three shillings, as a proper souvenir of Coronation Day. Step closer, gentlemen. . . ."

Cissy thought a smile twinkled in his eyes for a moment, but she couldn't be sure.

"He knows us, Frank. Pa must have left his jail door unlocked on purpose like he sometimes does. But to stand up *here* and preach! Oh, I want a Bible for a souvenir, I do! I never saw a Bible save the big one chained to the pulpit in church. They say it be words from God! Frank, I must have a Bible!"

"No! What do you think Pa would say? Only Dissenters have Bibles."

"I have a right to some of the money, and I will spend it the way I please! Pa doesn't have to know."

"A Bible! Do you fancy you'll preach too?"

"A Bible for the gentleman, a wise choice." Master Bunyan smiled widely and held out the book to Cissy. "And if you are short of coin today, this shall be a gift," he said to her in a gentler tone.

"Pay in true, lest he discover us," Frank said in her ear.

"I can pay, sir." Cissy handed up three shillings. "I thank you for your kindness."

He laughed heartily and turned his attention to other folk who were holding out their money for Bibles. Cissy wrapped the book in a handkerchief and hid it under one arm. "Don't you tell," she said. "I'll only look at it when Pa is downstairs collecting tolls. Wait a bit; I want to hear what he has to say."

Master Bunyan seemed satisfied that his street congregation was large enough. Opening one of the Bibles, he began to preach.

"You say this Book be only paper and ink," he began. "But it is a Book that is *alive!* The proof that this is the Word of God lies in its power to change a person's life. It changed me. Once I went to Divine Service twice a day, and every Sabbath Sunday. I loved the music, the incense, the rituals and play-acting. Yet it did not change me.

"I led a most wicked life. I could outcurse the meanest jack-tar from off the ships. One day while playing ball on the green, I seemed to hear God saying, 'Will you have your sins, or will you have heaven?'

"The call awakened my soul, and I saw what a priceless treasure was my soul, that it would spend eternity with its Maker, or without Him."

Cissy listened, and a horror of great loss began to seep into her mind. My soul, she thought. I have a soul that will live forever, that will outlive even my body. My soul may be kept or lost, as he says.

Master Bunyan went on, his powerful voice drawing in people from all around and holding them silent. "Then I tried to make myself righteous. I gave up everything, even dessert at mealtime. I thought that in the whole of England no man pleased God better than I did. I was fair pleased with myself. I was a painted hypocrite, though men called me godly. I was like a counterfeit coin!"

Now even Frank was interested, his eye fastened on the farmer with hay sticking out of his boots.

"That wasn't the way to salvation!" cried Master Bunyan. "For I fell into worse sin than before. When temptations came, I couldn't stand. I was like a pig that washed itself and then returned to the mud. *Because I wasn't any different within!*"

Aye, he speaks true and looks right into my own life, thought Cissy. For if I were good within and in favor with God, I would have the courage to say no to lawbreaking.

Bunyan went on: "One day I saw a toad croaking in a puddle, and I thought he was happier than I. For three years I was up and down, up and down; quiet in my soul one day, then in fear the next. I had no peace.

"One day as I walked in the field, this sentence flashed into my mind: *Thy righteousness is in heaven.* Then I saw that Jesus Christ at God's right hand was my righteousness—no matter how I felt.

"Jesus, only Jesus. Not myself. In Him I stand at God's right hand. Jesus Christ, the same yesterday, today, forever. He is calling you today. Will you follow Him?"

Cissy stood silent as a statue. Righteous. Pure and holy. Could that be said of her? Though the air was warm and her vest heavy, she shuddered.

Frank put his arm around her shoulder. "Pay him no mind— frightening good churchgoing people so's he can sell them Bibles. He should stick to tinkering. We must dispose of this coin quickly, so let's have a bite to eat down the block at the Poets and Writers Nook."

They paid for their meal in false and received change in true. They bought a side of meat from a butcher for Peg, paid in false, pocketed the true. Cissy picked out three bolts of cloth and a new set of bobbins from Flanders, carved and decorated with beads. They hired a small boy to carry all the bundles.

"Here's a penny for yourself, boy." Frank grinned at the small urchin and handed him the parcels.

Cissy bought a pearl pin and a pair of silver buckles from one merchant, scissors and colored threads from a seamstress.

"Buy a small item; give a large coin," Frank instructed her. "Degrooter has people in all the English towns passing his coin. Don't forget to get everything on the list Peg gave you."

Cissy nodded unhappily. "Do we ride back tomorrow?"

"Up before dawn to get a good start."

She walked along mechanically, the happiness gone out of her day. Jesus was calling, Master Bunyan said—he that was willing to lie in cold, damp Bedford Jail rather than in a feather bed in his own home. Jesus was calling. The only Jesus she knew had a crown of thorns and mournful eyes with circles underneath them. Jesus, ascending to heaven on a pink-edged cloud, as she'd seen him once in a painting. Jesus had somehow called to Master Bunyan, and Master Bunyan had become a new man. The Prayer Book spoke of Jesus' love, but it didn't explain anything.

Cissy went through the motions of buying, paying, and handing the bundles to the errand boy, but one great yearning swelled in her heart and repeated itself over and over: *Oh, if only He would call me—how gladly would I run after Him!*

The Highwayman

Cissy dreaded returning to Bedford Jail. The only thing that helped her feel better was the thought of seeing Master Bunyan again. And the Bible hidden in her saddlebag.

They rode hard the afternoon of the second day, anxious to cover twenty miles before dark and reach Luton. Frank carried the pistol he purchased in London and assured Cissy that she was as safe in his company as in her own bed at home.

"I'm wishing myself there," she complained. "I'm always afeared going through the Dell."

They turned left at a fork in the road and headed toward the sunset. After riding for half an hour past limestone cottages and flocks of sheep, Frank reined in his horse, smiling lamely. "Cissy, stop a bit. We must go back to the fork and take the right turn."

Cissy showed her alarm. "Nay, we be on the right road. It's getting dark; we can't turn back now. We could stop at a farmhouse."

"Turn back!" Frank yanked his horse around. "Master Greave's place is somewhere around, and he expects us. We won't find the Dell in this direction. Do you fancy spending the night in a tree?"

Cissy hesitated. "Are you certain?"

"May the earth open up and swallow me if I tell not the truth! We do wrong to be riding west."

"Foxed, by my own brother," Cissy retorted. "Next time I'll ride with the village milkmaid."

"While we bide here, it grows darker," Frank reminded her.

"Well, vexed I am, for it's worse for a female to be approached than for a man! Let's turn then, and hurry."

In the lavender twilight they reared their horses around to face the opposite direction. As they passed the crossroads Cissy saw a roughly built gibbet, where a lawbreaker, long dead, hung from a rope, his body tarred to preserve it from the weather.

A warning for me, she thought. To her brother she said, "Wouldn't it be better to ride back to Hertford?"

"Much too far. Here's the right turn, and the horse will know the way through the Dell. Full moon tonight." He paused. "Still, all that coin in the bags, true coin worth full price. Pa would be almost killing us were we robbed."

Cissy shivered and urged her horse ahead. Twisted trunks of beech trees warned them they were entering the Dell. She spied the moon between the branches, like a white swan caught in the rushes. The Dell was dark with shadows, and they descended deeper and deeper down a sloping hill.

They rode single file, Cissy first and Frank just behind, his horse's head almost bumping her elbow.

"Fall back," Cissy said over her shoulder. "Don't ride so close, Frank; the path is narrow."

"Fall back?" A strange man's voice mocked her; a hand seized her horse's bridle. "Nay, Mistress Nidd—Cissy—I'll not fall back."

"Frank!" Cissy fought to wrench the bridle back into her control as her horse tried to rear. She had to plunge both hands into its mane to keep from sliding off. A highwayman! And he knew her name! Knew, maybe, that they were carrying money!

The stranger soothed the horse until it stayed quiet. "Ride on into the clearing beyond, Cissy Nidd. Your brother will follow shortly."

Should she risk a run for it? No, the Dell was too cluttered with tree roots and low bushes underfoot. Had he stabbed Frank and left him to die? She began to shake so that she all but fell from the saddle.

How did the Prayer Book go? 'Twasn't often she looked into it, but parts of it fell into place. "God of all mercies . . . something something . . . defend Thy child from . . . from the evils and perils of the sea. . . ." No, that wasn't right—

The highwayman laughed. "What, praying against me? Nay, Cissy, I'll not harm you nor touch the money you bring from London in your saddlebags—not if you'll walk with me in the moonlight."

They entered the clearing on level ground; he dismounted, rolled a boulder closer, and anchored the horses' bridles under it. Then he held out his hand. "Come, Mistress Nidd."

"N-n-no, sir; I pray you have mercy. I am but a girl."

"My word upon it, I will not harm you. The word of a highwayman."

"Frank—my brother—"

"He is safe, I tell you. Will you not take my arm and we shall stroll a bit, Cissy? Come, now." His hand on her arm was light, as a gentleman's should be. He lifted her down from the horse.

"Good sir, take the money and welcome. Only let us go our way."

"You be lost. Do you remember this clearing on your way to London?" he asked.

"N-no," she said. "No, we passed no clearing in the Dell, only a long path by a stream."

"You see? Providence sent me to guide you. I know of Master Greave's house, and you should have skirted the clearing and kept it on your left hand."

Cissy felt a rush of relief. "I—I thank you, I do, and if you let me join my brother, we will go directly. He will pay you for your kindness," she added quickly.

The man laughed and unmasked himself. Cissy saw a longish face, deep dimples on each side of a thin, shaven chin, and straight brown hair to just below his ears.

"I claim a forfeit instead," he said gaily. "Play the grand lady to my gentleman."

She trembled even more and kept her head bent. Gently he reached for the boy's cap that hid her hair. "Cissy, will you not let me turn you into a lady? Let down that hair, that blood red hair that matches your lashes."

"Oh, no, no—please, it's such trouble to do it up!"

He dropped his hand. "I would not force you."

She looked at him with less fear. "How do you know me?"

"Walk with me in the moonlight and you shall find out."

Slowly, slowly, she pulled off the cap and unbraided her hair and shook it around her shoulders.

"Can you pace a minuet, if I hum a tune?"

"Could I learn a minuet living in a jail house?" she returned, watching his face.

"Pardon me, I forgot. You have danced at village fairs, have you not?"

She turned her face away. "Pa never lets me go anywhere."

"Just as well, they're bawdy affairs."

He lifted the tips of her fingers. "Then we shall have just a romantic stroll and get acquainted. I shall teach you court manners, and when you are invited to meet the queen at Whitehall, you shall stand with the best of them."

"For shame, to mock me!"

"I would not mock you, little Cecelia Nidd. Hark now, you must learn the songs of the day: *Go and catch a falling star; Fa-la-la-de-dum,*" he sang in a low voice. His hand held hers, but she did not feel at all imprisoned.

"I heard that line in a coffee house," he went on. "And there's more: *Gather ye rosebuds while ye may. . . .* I can't remember the rest. Ends with 'summer-o,' I think. Ah, Cissy, your hair glows like dark coals of garnet. Stand up straight; you have a way of slumping with your shoulders. Look a body in the face. That's better, love. You have beautiful eyes, and those slashing brows darken them and make them shine. There's no life in the eyes, though. Pray smile, Cissy, dear."

"No, you are bold." She pulled her hand away, and he did not move.

"Now here's a pretty song; mark the title—'To Celia.' *Drink to me only with thine eyes, and I will pledge with mine.* That's the only favor I ask tonight, Cissy Nidd."

With a swift movement he swung his cloak off his shoulders and wrapped it around her. "There now, you look more like a woman should. Do you tire of my company?"

She covered her face with her hands and whimpered. The handsome stranger frightened her; yet she was attracted to him. Tears welled up in her eyes and wet her hands. "I w-want to go home, please."

He kept his distance. "Cissy, I will marry you in a year or two. Yes, I will marry you, Cissy Nidd."

"You—a highwayman!"

"I'll not be a highwayman then, my love. I study architecture on the side. The robbing game pays for my schooling. Someday I will build! Oh, I do want to build things, Cissy. I have such ideas! Buildings that will be taller, scrape the sky maybe, get those chimney tops higher so the city isn't sooty and dark. I have ideas for a great tower to honor God, with windows all around and spires and crosses. Mayhap He then will find it in His heart to forgive my past."

Cissy couldn't help smiling. Why, he was young, and quite honorable, and certainly would be respected. She drew several deep breaths and wiped her sweaty hands on her breeches.

"No, I'll not be a highwayman much longer. I have money put by, and we can cross over to France or Holland and marry."

Without even so much as a *By your leave,* thought Cissy. Aloud she said, "How do you know me?"

"I have come to Bedford Jail many times, late at night, even after the gates close, coming up under the jail in a small boat. Wicket pays me, you know. Yes, I work for your Pa. How do you think you two young pea pods could travel to London and back, carrying money, and not be molested save I be watching from a distance? Oh, I'd do battle for you, Cissy!"

He smiled. "I have seen you by the fireside at Bedford Jail, working on your lace with nobody to confide in but your cat, Tabby. Once I was early and picked the lock on the cellar door. The prisoners were snoring away most manfully, and I came around to the foot of the stairs by the barred door. I heard Wicket speaking to you; harsh and unloving he was, and I feared for you. He's always had a cruel streak. Your mother's death struck him hard."

"I was but four," Cissy said quickly. "It wasn't my fault. She drowned in the river, saving me."

"Of course it wasn't your fault. Cissy, does he ever strike you with his fist?"

"No," she half-whispered, "he does it with words."

"Ah, poor darling."

"Does my father know how you talk to me?" Her voice came out sounding strained and afraid.

"Not he!" The highwayman laughed. "I'm sure you know of his plans for you and Paul Cobb. I have laughed ever since I heard of it. You're still too young, Cissy. Do you wait for me, for I'll marry you, I will. Now aren't you wondering my name, the name that shall be yours on that day?"

"I don't know your name, no."

He leaned against a sapling, and she saw his silhouette against the moon. "Gil Turpin."

"Oh, I do know the name! The king has a price on your head! Gil Turpin! You could be that awful tarred body back there swinging at the crossroads!"

Gil smiled broadly. "Why, Mistress Nidd, do you care?"

She made no reply.

"I am much encouraged," he continued. "I will not be caught, Cissy, for Charles II enjoys hearing of my pranks, though he nods in the direction of the law."

Cissy clasped her hands together in misery for his danger. "Now I recall; I saw in London a poster heralding your name and deeds. That you are a gallant highwayman who often shares the money with the less fortunate or returns half to the one robbed. But you are still afoul of the law, a criminal."

She took a few steps toward him, then stopped, seeing his expression.

"And what is Wicket Nidd?" he said coolly. "And you, Cissy Nidd, are you not part of it?"

She began to cry and stumbled toward her horse, reached it and tugged on the bridle. "You only wanted some amusement, somebody to tease. Now let me go; you've had your game."

"Stay, Cissy! Hear me. This life of a highwayman won't last, I say; then I'll have more money than I could earn in ten years at a trade. I've never harmed a soul. Go, then, if you will. Frank is waiting at the fork in the road. Master Greave's house is just a ten-minute ride."

He strode toward her. "Let me help you to mount, but before I do. . . ." He searched inside a vest pocket and held up a thin, glittering necklace of gold that had a dark red jewel dangling from it.

"Will you let me fasten it around your neck—and you keep it well hidden? This seals my promise, Cissy."

She moved as if in a dream, lifting her heavy hair, feeling his kiss on her forehead.

"A ruby to match your hair." He stepped back. "I have no right to give more, nor you to respond. Can you mount yourself? Of course, for you do ride well."

She mounted, dropped his cloak down to him, then turned her horse in the clearing and started down the path. Ahead of her she saw her brother emerge, smiling, from a clump of beech trees. As he waved her on, it occurred to her that Frank had been very cooperative to wait out of sight!

Cissy turned only once. She saw Gil Turpin standing in the moonlight in the clearing, his head thrown back, laughing at her.

Swan Inn

At home, alone in her little room, with the boys gone and Pa in the next town on business, Cissy searched out her little oval mirror of polished metal. She used it to examine herself piece by piece, trying to put together the reflection of a jailer's daughter. Oh, why was Pa angry that she had a mirror? So she couldn't see how she was growing? Or was he afraid she'd find something in herself to admire?

Were it not for the ruby that glowed at her throat, she thought she might have dreamed the meeting in the Dell with Gil Turpin.

She leaned out over a small windowsill and looked at the yellow birdhouse by the lilac tree. No wren would ever nest there, although it once had been built for a wren. In the middle of May, Frank had whispered a few words to her one night before supper. "Tonight—look in the yellow birdhouse."

Cissy had found Gil's note poked in the doorway, hidden by wisps of hay. The next day she had replied with just a few lines, but after four more notes she kept a regular diary for him.

He must keep tabs on everything I do anyhow, she thought. He visits Pa after dark for his pay every week. She looked at her face again in the hand mirror. Would she really be presented to the queen someday, married to a famous architect?

Well, not the English queen, she answered herself. For they would live in France or Holland.

Dreamily she turned from the window, thrusting a folded piece of paper into her apron pocket. This note was from Master Bunyan to his wife, and Cissy had agreed to take it to her. Cissy had never met Mistress Bunyan. She supposed the woman would be stern and worried looking, what with four little ones hanging on to her skirts, and her husband in jail.

Cissy left the house, still thinking about Gil. When would she see him? His notes bulged out the binding of her Bible, but notes weren't enough. She was still too young, he said. She must be patient.

She walked past the grammar school and St. Paul's church, past houses and cornfields and ditches.

Cissy could hear the soft hum of spinning wheels and the clack-clack of hand looms through open doorways. Looking in the window of the Apothecary Shop, she saw Master Whipple busy at a table, mixing potions.

"Good morning to you, Cissy. Do you need a cure?" Master Whipple dried herbs and roots and stored them in wooden barrels. His shelves held bottles of all sizes filled with liquids of all hues.

"Good morning, Master Whipple. No, thank you, I don't need medicine. I am quite well and on my way to the Bunyan home."

"Ah, a brave woman Mistress Bunyan is, for all she's married to a thoughtless man who risks their very home by defying the church. Cissy, you're peaked and pale from working too hard at your lace. Methinks your Pa should send you on an errand oftener, to get you out into the sunshine."

He chattered on. "If I didn't know you were but fifteen, I'd say you were in love. Turned-down mouth and slow step—I know the signs. Aha! Cissy Nidd in love! Bless my soul, there's a thought for you. Bear my greetings to Mistress Bunyan and say I'll not charge her a farthing for potions."

"I'll do so." Cissy passed Master Oates, who ran a pawn-shop. John Fennes, friend of Master Bunyan, was a hatter. The clog maker had hung a stout wooden shoe over his doorway.

Past the center of town, facing the church, stood a small thatched-roof cottage with a high chimney. At the bottom of the garden, a tinker's shanty leaned against a tree. The Bunyan door was open to let in the breeze, but Cissy knocked politely. She heard the children out back shouting and bouncing a ball. She was not at all prepared for the girl in a plain green gown with merry brown eyes who ran out and threw her arms around her neck and kissed her. Betsy Bunyan, plump as a milkmaid, had a dimpled chin and rosy face.

"Mistress Nidd! Please come in and have a cool drink, do! Honored I am to have you visit. How is my husband, pray?"

"He sent you a note. I'm just Cissy, Mistress Bunyan."

"And I'm just Betsy." Eagerly she opened the folded paper, read it, and burst into laughter. "Oh, my dear, listen to this from a man in prison despairing of his very life!

> *The frog by nature is but damp and cold,*
> *Her mouth is large, her belly much will hold.*
> *She sits somewhat ascending, loves to be*
> *Croaking in gardens, though unpleasantly."*

Cissy's eyes widened, unbelieving. "Is that all he says?"

Betsy laughed again, referred to the note, and blushed. "No, there be a little more, but it's just for me. Cissy, do come in for a spell."

"I can't stay. Pa . . . "

Betsy rushed on. "Cissy, will you go with me at noon to the Swan Inn? The judges are dining there, and I shall march in and make another appeal for my John. The trip to London brought no action; so I'm obliged to appeal again."

"Have you been all the way to London?" Cissy followed her into the room and sat on a stool. Betsy ran out, returning with a pitcher of ice-cold buttermilk from the cold cellar.

"Yes, 'deed I have, and all for nothing." Betsy served up half a stale gooseberry tart on a faded brown plate. "Oh, but Brother Fenne has been right good about sending milk, and Sister Tilney sends bread each day. Our garden thrives, and even poor blind Mary, only nine years old, picks beans and tomatoes. As you know, she takes her father a jug of soup every day, and one of the boys guides her so she can learn to go alone."

Cissy looked around curiously. The room was bare but clean, the hearth neat with a pile of firewood to one side. Betsy's big stuffed pillow, identical to Cissy's work pillow, sat plumped on a stool. The bobbins hung down and the finished lace was rolled up on a clean stick and covered with a cloth.

It sounds as if the other Dissenters are taking good care of them, Cissy thought. She drank the buttermilk, feeling guilty that she was taking it from the children. Betsy filled her mug again. "Goodness! You're just a child, Cissy! Are you fourteen?"

"Almost sixteen."

Betsy sat down on the other wicker chair. "I'm twenty. You asked if I've been to London. Yes, Brother and Sister Fenne took me. Oh, the people! Thick as weeds in the poorhouse garden! I saw a woman with bare feet a-smoking a man's pipe, rooting in an oyster barrel for something to eat! One vender cried, *'Diddle, diddle, dumpling; Dumplings-ho!'* And right there on the street, Master Fenne bought us hot dumplings!" Betsy laughed in delight.

You could out-chatter a magpie, you could, Cissy thought, but she couldn't help smiling back at Betsy.

"Ah, I made you laugh! What a pretty girl you are when you smile!" Betsy caught up the little boy who toddled through the doorway and smothered him with kisses. "My darling, can you not play without falling into the stream? My sweet little ducky, mind Mary and Elizabeth lest you stray away from the yard."

She put the child down. "Cissy dear, will you go with me at noon? 'Twould be your chance to see fine gentlemen at table, and the beautiful inside of the Swan Inn."

"I look at the outside of Swan Inn every day, seeing it's just across from the jail. What should I wear?"

"What you have on is just fine. My Sabbath dress is at the pawnshop again, but I have money to redeem it for today. That will be the third time this year I have paid for that frock! I'm most 'shamed to face the man again; he thinks me a bold baggage! But for John's sake I'll do it."

Cissy thought of Master Bunyan lying on straw in his dirty cell with the river rushing underneath, sending its dampness up through every crack in the floor. "Yes, I'll go with you, even though I'll be bashful in front of the gentlemen," she said. "When you made the appeal in London, what did you do?"

"I went right into the House of Lords with a petition for Lord Barkwood, as my husband instructed me. His lordship said it was out of his jurisdiction and that I must return to my own county and wait for the judges to sit."

"And they sit formally today at dinner?"

Betsy nodded. "Yes. Yesterday John wrote up another petition, and when Judge Twisden rode into town in a coach I stood by the road and curtsied and threw the petition in the window."

Cissy was startled. "You dared to do that? And did he see it?"

"See it? It struck him on the nose! Such a red, bulbous nose he has. He stuck his head out and bawled some profanity and rode on. Cissy, have you ever seen a coach?"

"I saw the gold coaches with big wheels drawn by six horses on Coronation Day." Silently she asked, And would you like me as much did you know what I was doing there?

"Oh," Betsy said, "this is a coach that carries gentlemen about in a small town. It's like a casket with a domed roof, swaying along like a ship at sea. Did I ever have to ride one, I'd jump out and swim for dry land!"

Cissy laughed. "Will you take the children along with you?"

"What a splendid idea! 'Twould shame them for fair! Judge Twisden, Judge Hale, and Justice Chester will be there. They deserve to be pinched black and blue, those three! Master Blind-man, Master Malice, and Master Hate-light, I call them, for their judgments against the poor. I met Judge Hale once, and he wasn't too sharp with me. May God forgive me, we must love our enemies, but to condemn a man to jail because he has been a comfort to hundreds of people. . . . Ah, I can't bear to think on it; I would think such unchristian thoughts! Cissy, my John has powerful enemies.''

"How so?''

"King Charles II is now crowned king after his exile, you know. In June a petition was presented in the House of Lords, a petition for John's permanent arrest. Under strict conditions, Cis-sy. Not an arrest like he has now, with the kindness of your Pa leaving the door unlocked every once in a while. And John's honesty in coming back to jail after he's been out preaching in disguise.''

It's the only kindness I ever knew in Pa, thought Cissy. Master Bunyan plays a good game of chess; mayhap that's the answer. It's not often that Pa can find someone to spend an evening over a game board.

"John once preached in Cambridge, in the big cathedral, before his arrest. So you see, even the king knows of my husband.''

"I know naught of such things.'' Cissy grew uncomfortable listening to talk against royalty.

"The king issued the Declaration of Breda: 'Liberty to tender consciences and amnesty for all those excluded by Parliament.' Only pretty words, for the king never kept that promise.''

The mention of the new king made Cissy think of Gil Turpin. Gil had said the king called him ''Swift Nicks'' and laughed at his doings. Were Gil caught, Parliament might press for his execution.

She forced her thoughts back to Betsy. ''I will run home and set out the dinner for the men,'' she said. ''You visit the pawn-shop, and I will meet you here within the hour.''

After the meal was ready, Cissy washed her hands and face, took off her apron, and met Betsy back at the Bunyan house.

Together they climbed the steps of the Inn, followed by the children, who held hands and led blind Mary along. Betsy wore a black dress with white collar and cuffs. Her hair was brushed into a knot at the back of her head, and not a single ringlet showed.

Swan Inn on the River Ouse showed a sign out front, a giant white swan on a dark background. One swan to represent the hundreds that nested on little inlets of the river.

What if Pa should look out the window at this minute, Cissy thought. What if he should happen to look across the river just now?

The judges were dining in Swan Chamber, a servant told them, looking them over with a frown. Betsy knocked at the door of the chamber, and a maid in black opened to them. Cissy saw a room of high oaken beams and dark paneled walls. She knew the Inn was built out over a pier at the water's edge.

Before the maid could shut the door, Betsy cried out, "Judge Hale, your honor, allow me a word, only a word for the sake of justice!"

Cissy had heard that Judge Hale was reported to be kindly to Dissenters. She had often heard him criticized for it after Divine Services on Sunday. The judge beckoned them in. Robed in ermine and scarlet and powdered wigs, the three men sat at a banquet table big enough for twenty. The squires and burgesses of Bedford sat around a smaller table and kept a respectful quiet.

Betsy addressed Judge Hale. "My lord, I come again to ask if you can do anything for my husband."

Judge Hale dipped up his soup with a silver spoon. The table almost sagged under the weight of serving dishes and platters, rabbit pie, and sausage pudding. Cissy recognized the aroma of gingered chicken, for she had once made it at Christmas time. She saw a huge leg of mutton, platters of fish, and a lettuce salad as big as a bushel basket. She smelled kidney pie and fried oysters.

Methinks they will have the stomachache by and by, she thought. That food would feed 'most all of Bedford's poor.

Judge Hale stopped eating long enough to use an ivory tooth picker. "My good woman, your husband has been convicted by law. What can I do?"

"My lord, it was unlawful. He was never even asked whether he was guilty or not. And he did not confess to any guilt. The most he did was preach the Word of God and pray at several meetings. God's blessing was upon those meetings; the people bore witness to that truth."

Cissy stood unnoticed, partly hidden by the drapery at the windows, and she listened, marveling at Betsy's boldness.

Judge Twisden scowled from behind the leg of fowl he was devouring. "Your husband, woman, is a breaker of the peace."

"He was not lawfully convicted," repeated Betsy.

"Bring the Statute Book," said Judge Hale to one of the squires.

Justice Chester, in a curly wig stiff with sugar water, looked at Betsy with scorn. "He *was* lawfully convicted, for I presided at the trial."

Judge Twisden turned to the man seated next to him. "The cook here is French. Mark how the leg of mutton is laid over with sugared oranges and plum jam, and the fish with a nice sop of butter and honey."

"There are times when I'm not certain what 'tis I am eating. Methinks the French way is too sweet for my palate."

How can they eat and eat, Cissy wondered, when families in Bedford go hungry? Such delicacies were seen on her table only at holiday times.

"My lord," Betsy began again, her face pale and serious, "the House of Lords let me believe they had committed my husband's release to the judges here. You give me no satisfaction one way or the other."

"Be that woman still here?" Judge Twisden, who had a raw, fleshy face, tipped his head back to drink. Every time he moved, powder fell off his wig into the food. "Will your husband leave off preaching and stick to tinkering?"

"He dare not, as long as he has a tongue in his mouth."

Judge Twisden turned to Judge Hale. "My lord, he is a pest, the worst in all of England. Send her away, do."

Betsy pushed the little ones forward a little. "My lord, I have four small children that cannot help themselves, of which one is blind. We have nothing to live upon but the charity of some good people. Winter is coming on."

"You parade your poverty to get sympathy," sneered one of the squires.

Judge Hale laid down his knife and sipped from a crystal goblet. "You are young to have four."

"They are my husband's, and his wife is dead. I have been married less than two years. My own babe died at birth."

"Alas, poor woman!" Judge Hale stared at her kindly, then wrapped four bonbons in a napkin. "Take these, for the children."

Bonbons! thought Cissy angrily. They may starve to death this winter, and he gives them each a sweet to whet their appetites.

"Thank you." Betsy accepted them graciously.

"I will send you venison each month, and a sugar loaf," said Judge Hale in a lower tone meant only for Betsy's ears, but Cissy heard.

"What is your husband's trade?" he asked in a louder voice.

"A tinker! A tinker!" cried the squires of Bedford from their table nearby.

"Aye," Betsy retorted promptly, "and because he is but a poor tinker, he cannot get justice!"

In a temper, Justice Chester snatched off his wig and scratched his bald head. "He was convicted! He was convicted!"

"There are only three things to do," said Judge Hale gently. "You must apply yourself to the king again. Or, you may ask for a full pardon from him. Or, you may get a writ of error, claiming the law was in error."

"But he was lawfully convicted!" cried Justice Chester. He scraped back his chair, and Cissy thought he would lean forward and strike Betsy with his fist. "He insists upon preaching and prating and does anything he pleases!"

"He preaches nothing but the Word of God," said Betsy calmly.

Aye, that he does, thought Cissy. In London he preached God's words right into my heart, and I have been reading my Bible ever since.

Justice Chester was breathing quickly, in a rage. "That country bumpkin preach the Word of God? An ignorant tinker? A mender of pots and pans? Do you know how long a clergyman studies theology? Ten years! Your husband's doctrine is of the devil!"

"Send her away!" bellowed Judge Twisden.

"Do you forget where you are?" Judge Hale frowned him down. "Don't take on so before the other men. Mistress Bunyan, I cannot help you, poor soul. I suggest you get a writ of error."

"There was no error! He was lawfully convicted!" Justice Chester upset his water glass, and a servant sprang forward with a napkin and mopped him down in the front.

All the men fell to quarreling, and Betsy motioned the children out of the room. Cissy followed them, wondering how a poor person who could not afford a legal man might get justice.

Outside, Betsy threw her hands across her face and burst into tears, sobbing wildly.

"Pray don't cry, Betsy." Cissy led her downstairs, supporting her. "You will find a way to help Master Bunyan."

But she couldn't imagine how, and her heart felt heavy as a tombstone.

Out on the wide porch of the Swan Inn, Betsy cried on while the children held onto her gown, frightened. "I'm not crying for him," Betsy said weeping, "nor for the children, nor for myself."

She wiped her eyes with her kerchief. "Ah, those men! What hardhearted creatures! Poor things, what will they say on the

Judgment Day when they must explain all the deeds done and the words said? How will they answer?'' She fell to weeping afresh.

Cissy hugged her close and thought, she hardly sees the plight of Master Bunyan nor her own hard life. She actually pities those wretches!

Trouble!

A letter a month, Cissy said to herself, counting the precious notes filed in the front of her Bible. Indeed, her Gil had honey on his tongue and wrote a most fine letter. *Cissy, my love, ever wear the ruby nearest your heart. This gem was purchased, on my honor, and paid for dearly with coin of the realm, sweetheart.*

The lingering autumn weather had favored trips back and forth to the birdhouse, and twice, brief meetings with Gil himself. But all too soon autumn was over and winter had set in. The bitterly cold days almost drove Cissy to despair. Pa seldom went out; his bones shrank from the cold, he claimed. The two brothers lazed about or worked on counterfeit coins. It was a rare treat to have the house to herself for a few hours like this so she could look over Gil's notes and read her Bible.

Cissy had slowly read her way through the Bible, from the very beginning, spelling out some of the long words and guessing at their meanings. Only when she was alone dared she take the Bible, wrapped in an old tablecloth, out of its hiding place far underneath her bed.

She pulled her shawl tighter and tucked her cold feet under each other on the hearth for warmth. Pa was that stingy with the coal! Outside, the River Ouse was flooding its banks. She could hear the water sloshing underneath the house, sending up its damp into all the rooms and forcing a layer of mud and water into the cellar of Bedford Jail.

Poor Master Bunyan, Cissy thought. Little enough there is I can do for him, except to take him extra victuals now and then. "Oh, I must take him something before the men get home," she exclaimed.

She ran up to her room and slid the Bible with Gil's letters back under the bed. Hurrying through the kitchen, she caught up two stale rolls and a heel of cheese, then slipped her feet into wooden clogs to keep them dry and took the jail key from its hook by the window.

Master Bunyan was pacing back and forth like a caged lion. He started at the sound of her footsteps and spun around. "Cissy Nidd! Pleased I am to see you, not having entertained company for a fortnight. I get the jumps on a day like this when the cell is damp and shadowy. I dread sundown in the winter. But I have a little pet now, and you may meet him shortly. Come in, come in, sit a spell."

He accepted the food gladly. "I thank you; that will taste good later on. Now don't move and I'll show you something." He tapped on the side of the hearth with a stick, and Cissy saw a black spider almost as big as a saucer slide himself through a crack.

> *"I hide myself*
> *When I for flies do wait.*
> *So doth the devil*
> *When he lays his bait."*

Cissy smiled faintly. "I fear he and I shan't be friends. I cannot stay this time; the men will be back shortly. I'll come back another time."

She locked his cell and hurried upstairs. Frank was waiting for her there, and he pulled her aside. He spoke softly. "You may expect a visitor tonight at half past eleven, Sis. Do be careful."

Cissy's heart almost stopped, then pounded like a shoemaker's hammer. "Tonight?" she whispered. "With the river in flood, and the cold?"

He nodded. "Not by the birdhouse, too watery out there. Step just outside the kitchen door and wait in the shadow. He shan't stay long. There's trouble."

"What trouble?" Cissy could scarcely get the words out. Then she heard the clomping of Pa's horse and Pa's loud voice.

"I thank you, Frank." She turned and quickly hung the jail key by the door.

"Where's the food?" Pa yelled, glaring at the empty table.

Cissy trembled and almost dropped the plate she had run to fetch. "I-I forgot. I mean, in winter I hardly know when 'tis supper; the sun doesn't seem to come up and go down like in summer. It's so dark all the time."

Pa threw his coat in a corner along with his woolen scarf. "Sometimes I wonder if you have a brain at all. Well, there's a rabbit skinned all nice in that bag of mine. Stew it in a hurry afore Harold gets back. I traded Master Hibbins some coal for one of his wife's fresh puddings. So you can thank me, ugly mug, that you won't starve to death!"

Cissy shut her eyes to the voice and fixed her thoughts on the fine meal they'd have. And then tonight! If only they'd go to bed early.

The meal was the best they'd had since the Christmas feast. The men ate so much there were no leftovers for the next day. Frank and Harold almost fell asleep at the table; they had worked hard digging out a stream to try to divert the river from flooding the jail.

Pa yawned and amused himself by practicing chess moves on a homemade board, but he soon gave up. "I'm right ready for bed this early, but no thanks to you," he told Cissy. "I don't want to hear any dish clattering or you a-hummin' or the fire snapping. I'm to bed, and you get straight upstairs this minute."

Cissy left the dirty dishes and pans on the table and went upstairs. She shut the door, sat on the bed, and hugged herself for joy. How well it had all worked out. Oh, the men would sleep like bears in a cave tonight, she knew. They always did when they were full of food.

She buried her head in her hands and waited. It was no hardship, she thought, waiting for the one you love. She didn't dare lie down lest she fall asleep. The town clock struck the hours, and the crier passed, calling, "All is well."

But all is not well, Cissy said to herself, if Frank said there is trouble. When eleven o'clock struck, she wrapped herself in her dark shawl and began to tiptoe down the stairs. One step at a time, then wait to hear the snores. Only one step. Oh! This one creaks! Can I step over it? No, I'd fall and roll down the rest. One step. Wait. One step.

She listened once more to the snores, all on different notes of the scale, then softly unlocked the kitchen door. She shut it behind her and waited on the top step. He was there already, so early!

"Cissy, my love!" He gripped her arms. "Are you safe here? Are you cold? Tell me you are all right."

She choked back nervous laughter and hid her face in his cloak. "Shhh, you can see I am all right—now!"

"You're too thin! Do you get enough to eat?"

"Oh, plenty. But I-I'm not always hungry. I miss you; I wish to see the end of Bedford Jail; I want to be gone."

"Not yet." He tipped her face up. "Cissy, do you love me true? Enough to wait longer?"

Wait longer. That was the trouble Frank spoke of, then. Yes, she could wait longer and longer.

She nodded, but tears came into her eyes. Her lips trembled. "Frank spoke of trouble, but I'll wait for you, Gil Turpin, yes I will."

"Worse than that. I must leave England for a while. I was betrayed by a so-called friend and almost arrested. Cissy, love, I must go over to Holland for a while."

"No, no! Holland?" It might as well be China or India, it seemed that far. "Take me with you, Gil! Tonight! I'll just walk away and leave my clothes and my Bible and your letters. . . ."

"No, Cissy, I have nothing to offer you. What would we do in Holland? Be gypsies? Live in the streets? I must finish my studies."

"I don't need an architect for a husband."

"You don't need a bandit, either. Soon I'll have enough money, and you will never have to pass false coin again, love. You're safe here, though it's not a pleasant life for you. I'll write every week."

"The birdhouse?"

"No, Dutch Billy will bring my letters."

"Dutch Billy?" Cissy stared at him, puzzled. "Who is that?"

"A friend. He'll give the notes to Frank." He smiled down at her. "Trust me, Cissy, and wait for me. Do you wear the ruby?"

"Always." She reached for it. "And even though I lose it or it be taken from me, Gil Turpin, we are as good as betrothed."

"You love me, then?"

"I love you, Gil Turpin." She couldn't even see his face through her tears. After one kiss he hugged her to him, then backed down the steps. "Go in, quickly," he called up. "Quickly!"

Cissy locked the kitchen door behind her and tiptoed up the stairs to bed. Gone, after only a minute. Gone to Holland. For how long? She'd forgotten to ask him. And Dutch Billy? She'd never heard of such a person in Bedford. He must be a Hollander with that name. And he'd have to travel back and forth to Holland to bring Gil's notes, wouldn't he?

Confused and feeling ill, she crawled underneath the quilt and tried to sleep. She heard the crier pass every hour, and just before dawn she fell asleep from weariness.

Weeks dragged by and no word came from Gil. The winter days weighed on her as heavily as the wet laundry she hung on a rope in the cellar. Cissy washed clothes often, since the men went hunting rabbits and birds every other day. She used hot water from an iron kettle that stood on a stone platform, heated by a fire of coals. Cissy scrubbed, then wrung out the trousers and shirts as best she could. Her feet were never dry and her nose dripped like a fountain.

The prisoners were quiet, too cold and damp to make any noise. They squatted in corners, or hugged themselves for warmth, or marched up and down to stir the blood as Master Bunyan often did. From the narrow cellar window, Cissy could see across the snowy ground and partway into his cell. His suntan had faded, leaving him with a pale prisoner's face.

Thankful I am that Pa likes him, Cissy thought, wringing out Harold's smelly shirt. She spoke to the cat, for there was no other company. "Tabby, you should see Master Bunyan's cell. He has only a little fire grate, a lamp, and a rosebush in a pot. Drafty it is, too, with the few coals Betsy sends."

Tabby purred and curled into a circle, wrapping her long tail around her nose.

"Cissy! You—Cissy!"

Cissy hurried to string out all the washed clothes on the rope. If she didn't answer, maybe he'd call one of the boys for the errand. She coughed and wheezed, and warmed her red, swollen hands over the fire. The backs of them were cracked and bleeding.

"You—ugly mug! Where are you? Get along upstairs. I hear you a-sneezing down there!"

Cissy warmed her cold nose with her hands. "I'd best go up," she told Tabby. "Else he'll come down searching."

All the clothes were washed; so she scraped the live coals out from under the kettle and beat them with a stick to put out the flame and save them for the next time.

"Cissy-y-y-y! If I come down to fetch you, you'll rue the day!"

Cissy hurried up the back steps that led to the pantry where her father knelt, measuring out rye flour from a sack. "You're using up the flour too fast. I can tell. And I know you must be giving bread away. That's got to stop. Who are you feeding?"

Cissy wrapped one painful hand in her apron and didn't answer. She'd ask Goody to find some cobwebs to heal her sores.

Pa tied up the mouth of the sack and set the pan of rye flour on the floor. "Sit down on the stool yonder. I'll not fuss with you nor beat a path around the parson's bush, so to speak. I'll tell you right out. You're to marry Paul Cobb, come summer."

"Oh, no, Pa, please—it's too soon. I'll be but seventeen."

A vein rose and pulsed in his forehead. "Too soon? You should have been wed long ago. I can't feed you any longer."

Cissy felt hot and dry as though she'd been smoked in a chimney like a side of bacon. "P-pa, why must it be Paul Cobb? I can't abide the sight of him. I don't like him."

"Hold your tongue! Did I ask what you liked? Master Cobb has asked me for your hand, and the banns will be read in church. You could do worse than marry a townsman like him, with a house and land and income. You should bless your good fortune—and my goodness in allowing it!"

Cissy stiffened. Her teeth nipped the tip of her tongue, and she felt her heart quake within her. "No, Pa, I can't. Don't read the banns."

"You be out of your wits, with an impudent tongue. You haven't cast your cap for some other man, have you?"

"Oh, there's no one in the whole town I'd fancy!"

"Why he would pick such a wry-mouth I'll never understand." Pa tied the mouth of the sack shut and began to count the bunches of herbs hung overhead. "He wants you, and he has to have his way."

"Why?"

Pa glared at her over the sacks of rye and barley, his eyes wild and frightening. He lowered his voice to a rasping whisper.

"Because he found out—he knows about the coin, and should he tell, we'll all hang. We made a pact of silence, girl. He'll have you to wife."

Cissy felt a rush of sickness in her throat. She sat down on a low stool and locked her arms around her knees. Two painful choices faced her. And either way, she'd be hurt.

"Pa," she finally muttered, "tell him not 'til I'm twenty; this is too soon"

"Twenty! Who would marry a harpy as old as that?"

"Nineteen, then. Give me two more years, please, Pa."

Pa shook his head. "He wants you *now,* to dress you up fine and show you off. Now, while you're strong enough to cook and learn housekeeping."

Cissy caught desperately at his words. "I'm not strong, Pa; I haven't felt well for a long time. The coughs are worse, and every night I sit straight up in bed half the night afore I get to sleep."

"Bah! Everybody coughs when the fog is in. And I'll tell you more, my girl. You must marry Paul Cobb so you can help us should we be ruined. The king has ordered all new coin to be made with grained edges, so honest folk—such as we be—can't clip a bit off. I'll tell you more. By July coming, we must all turn our money in, accept less than it's worth, and begin to use the king's new currency."

"Then we'll be very, very poor?"

"You do see it plain, my girl. You may soon be the only way out of most miserable poverty for your family what's cared for you all these years and kept a roof over your head and a rag on your back. If we must give up clipping *and* passing false coin, we'll fair starve!"

Cissy twisted both hands in her apron to keep them still. "We be good as dead," she breathed, staring at him.

Her father returned the look without speaking. Then he said, "You sit there and think on it. Aye, we all be as good as dead unless you marry Paul Cobb!"

Thou Art My Love

Even after a week of applying cobwebs every day, Cissy's sore hands had not healed. "Keep them dry," Goody Pratt had said.

How could she, with all the work to be done? She rocked herself back and forth on the edge of her bed and cradled her hands in her apron. Ah, what woes are all around me, she mourned. What would Master Bunyan do? He has such peace in his soul, even lying in jail, cooped up like an owl in a hollow tree. He that loves the outdoors and mixing with all kinds of people and hiking about the countryside. How can he bear it?

And I have such misery in me and such troubles that reading the Prayer Book doesn't help, nor the Bible. I want to talk to Master Bunyan, I do. Maybe I could dish up some cabbage to give him when Pa goes out to collect tolls.

She hadn't long to wait. A horse and rider galloped up to the bridge, and the man called out in a hoarse voice. Cissy heard her father curse and stumble down the steps. Quick as a winged bird she ran to the fireplace, where a pot of leftover cabbage simmered. She ladled out a dish of cabbage and even found a piece of pork fat.

Pa never even bothered to lock Master Bunyan's cell, since he'd given his word he'd stay put for a while. Cissy ran down to ground level and opened the door of his cell.

"How be your spider?"

Master Bunyan swallowed the cabbage down in three gulps, supping it right up from the dish. "I thank you, Cissy; that was fit for an archbishop. Master Spider is fine. I have long conversations with him. When my eyes tire from writing my stories or making lace, I sit and talk to him."

Master Bunyan sat on one side of the hearth where a few coals glowed, and Cissy sat on the other side, far from the beloved spider.

Master Bunyan looked at her kindly. "Cissy . . ." he hesitated. "Cissy, how then is it with your soul?"

She knew he would ask. He spoke to everyone he met about God and sin and heaven. She had known before she came that he would ask her, and she wanted to talk to him.

"I attend Divine Service every month and read aloud in the Prayer Book along with the others."

"The Prayer Book!" exclaimed Master Bunyan. "Is it not against reason that a man many miles away should write a prayer to be read on a certain day next year? How does he know what my needs will be next year? Why must I repeat another man's prayer?"

Cissy drank in the words as though they were pure spring water. Such ideas he had! Such questions he awakened in her thinking. She had never been in a church different from her own. "How should we pray, if not from a book?"

"Pray with the spirit and with understanding. The Scriptures exhort us to do so," said Master Bunyan.

She avoided his eyes; they were so knowing. Surely he must know about the Nidd family and their doings. Mayhap God told him things. But of course he didn't know—what a foolish idea! He'd certainly preach a sermon at her if he did.

Master Bunyan added a few more of his precious coals to the fire."Cissy, my girl, I preach three main truths, and they are linked together. I oft depart from them onto other Bible subjects, but I always return to the three.

"First, the doom of the sinner without Christ.

"Next, the redemption by Christ on the cross.

"Then, the possibility of a close walk and talk with the Lord Jesus Christ by faith. The Christian life should be a romance, Cissy, a love affair with the Lover of our souls. Do you understand?''

Cissy wound a lock of her long hair around and around her thumb. She understood, in the sense that a heavy weight of guilt lay on her heart. She understood, as far as knowing that Christ died for the whole world. But she wasn't sure if she believed or not.

"No," she said, "I don't understand."

"Do you know the value of your soul and why its eternal loss would be so terrible? Cissy dear, your soul will live on and on forever, either with God or separated from Him."

A series of shivers seized her, and she hid her face in her hands. Oh, the honest folks she had cheated of their good coin . . . the lies to Pa . . . spiteful thoughts toward her brothers . . . hatred and disobedience. . . .

"I have guilt, yes. Oh, I do feel doom and fear, and it rises afore me so I don't see nor feel anything else. I be afeared of God."

"Thank God," Master Bunyan said, "for it is a sure sign God is calling to you. When God wishes to tune the soul to Himself, He often plays first upon the note of fear. No fears—no need of grace."

Cissy sat up, alert. Only that morning she'd read: *Noah . . . moved with fear . . . prepared an ark . . . to the saving of his house.* Then it wasn't wicked to fear.

Master Bunyan continued: "Oh, Cissy, cry to God to reveal Jesus Christ to you. There is none that can teach like Him! My poor words are like fluttering moths."

What would it mean for me to turn about and follow Him? Cissy thought. Her wretchedness began to increase. What would it mean to go Master Bunyan's way? Never again to pass false coin, to bear the wrath of her father and brothers, to refuse the love of a highwayman, to be a Dissenter and be persecuted, plagued, arrested, disgraced, jailed. No! She couldn't bear it!

Master Bunyan must have read her mind—she was sure of it, for he said, "The Lord gives grace, Cissy, and with more trial He gives more grace. Do you not wonder how I can bide here and not go mad when I think of Betsy and my four little ones? One day the Lord spoke this verse to me from Jeremiah 49:11, and all my fears for them fled: *Leave thy fatherless children, I will preserve them alive; and let thy widows trust in me.*"

"You were always a good man."

"You are mistaken there, Cissy. Once a harlot had to rebuke me, my speech was that foul. I could rap out an oath would make your heart terrified to hear it. I was as guilty as the counterfeiter's hand. For three years I was in conflict, not able to believe that God could forgive me."

"How did you change?"

"I heard a Dissenting pastor preach. He quoted from Solomon's Song, and it was God speaking to my soul: *Thou art my love.* Three times he said it: *Thou art my love.* Then I knew how much God loved me, not only enough to forgive, but enough to make me righteous."

"Righteous?" Cissy didn't understand.

"Not self-righteous, but accepted in Christ. The pastor told me to say it over and over whenever I doubted God loved me. For I was up and down; I had a nature that changed from day to day."

Master Bunyan gazed off into the distance. "*Thou art my love.* I tried to imagine God saying it to me, and at last I believed it. I stopped by a field of crows when I was walking one day and told them all about it, such was my joy."

"*Thou art my love,*" Cissy said softly.

"Say it again, as from God."

"*Thou art my love. Thou art my love,* says Almighty God."

"Cissy, if God is calling to your soul, don't turn away. Fall on your knees and let Him fill your life with peace and contentment. Jesus Christ has been more real than ever since I've been in prison."

Cissy sat without speaking, gazing into the mean little fire that gave so little warmth. She turned away her face so Master Bunyan could not read her thoughts. "I'll think on it," she said aloud.

"Cissy-y-y-y! Yoo-o-o-o!"

She stood up and reached for the empty dish. "Pa's calling. I think the townsmen are inspecting the jail today. There's still a chance you may be pardoned by the king, Master Bunyan. I heard Pa say your name is on that list."

He smiled slowly. "Yes, the laws change from day to day. A general amnesty has been proposed for all Dissenters. I truly am hopeful."

"Good day to you." Cissy closed the cell door behind her and ran through the snowy yard, up the steps to the pantry, and into the living room. Her father was setting stools and chairs around the fireplace.

"You there, Cissy! Call up Goody Pratt and Slade and Master Bunyan to work on bobbin lace, like model prisoners. The townsmen are calling today. Put on a clean pinafore. Pin up that stringy hair under a cap. Keep the fire low, and with luck they won't stay long because of the cold."

Cissy took the jail key off the hook and went to fetch the prisoners. Goody Pratt was aged and thin as a rush candle, wrapped in a dress that was once purple but now a gloomy black. Accused of being a witch, she had been caged in Bedford Jail until she would confess.

Since she could not remember why she was there, Cissy thought wryly, it wasn't likely she would ever get out. And where would she go? If she did confess, she'd be hung as a witch.

Slade was a simple-mind; just an old man with no home. He loved to read history books when he was fortunate enough to have an old one given him.

Cissy unlocked the door of the day room where men and women prisoners milled about together and motioned for Goody Pratt. She was one of their most clever lace makers. Though she'd forgotten all else, she had not forgotten her childhood spent in lace school.

"I'm a good woman, ain't I?" she said as Cissy pulled her through the crowd pressed against the jail door. "Dearie, say I'm a good woman."

"You're a good woman, Goody Pratt. Master Slade, you're to come up too and demonstrate lace making for the gentlemen."

Master Slade was as annoying as a wart. He had a mouth big enough to set in the forest to trap bears, Cissy had decided. She beckoned to Master Bunyan. The three prisoners followed her up the steps carrying their pillows, with the bobbins dancing off the sides.

They arranged themselves obediently around the fire and began to work on lace, knowing they would share in the refreshments. Cissy changed into a clean gown and pulled on dry stockings and slippers. She covered her hair with a starched cap and pulled it down almost to her eyebrows. Her dress was high-necked, and she draped a baggy shawl over it to conceal her figure. I'll make myself even uglier than I am, she thought, and maybe Paul Cobb won't notice me.

Her father looked at her sourly, but he said, "Now you look like a neat housewife instead of an unbroken colt, with that mop of hair covered up. Why can't you take pains to dress proper other times?"

Cissy arranged pewter mugs on the table and laid out slices of raisin and hazelnut cake on a platter.

Slade spied the feast out of the corner of one eye and chuckled and patted his middle. Goody Pratt smiled at the cake even while her fingers flew on the bobbins. Master Bunyan gazed gravely down at his work and said nothing.

"Cissy, allow the prisoners each a dry slice off the tail of the cake," Pa said.

Then they all heard the expected knock at the downstairs door. Cissy ran down to let the men in from the blowing hail. Paul Cobb and four other men stepped in, and Cissy curtsied to them and led the way upstairs.

She let her lower jaw hang slack, as Goody Pratt did, and kept her eyelids lowered. Maybe if she seemed as witless as a new-birthed rabbit, Paul Cobb would dislike her. Yes—that was it! She'd make him dislike her!

The men gathered around the table and helped themselves to drink and cake. Pa clasped and unclasped his hands, anxious to make a good impression.

To seal my fate, thought Cissy. She forced her shoulders to droop and let her tongue loll out.

Pa, catching sight of her, directed attention to the prisoners. "Gentlemen, here be three of our finest lace makers. They can turn out Italian, Belgian, or French lace. My own daughter— ahem, Paul—my own daughter can work a diamond pattern 'twould put her teacher to shame. I will have Cissy—ahem, Paul—I will have Cissy learn the new Flemish design and teach the prisoners. Quick as a cat's wink is my daughter. The other prisoners downstairs also work together in harmony. . . ."

A burst of raucous singing from below drowned out what he was saying. Pa turned red. "They're celebrating," he went on hastily. "Once a month they are allowed to celebrate . . . oh, they celebrate . . ." He turned desperately to old Slade. "What is it the prisoners celebrate on this day?"

Slade gladly neglected his lace making. "The king's birth-day—we be more than halfway to the king's birthday, which is April coming. His majesty, God bless 'im! A toast, gentlemen! Just fill up my cup again, if you please."

"His majesty!" they all echoed loudly.

Slade gulped his drink and held the cup up again hopefully. "His majesty, James the First!"

A dreadful silence spread in the room, and Cissy held her breath.

"To Charles II," Pa said unsteadily. "The prisoner is confused, his brain dead as an old winter turnip. Gentlemen, I give you our king!"

They filled the mugs over and over and began to talk of business and taxes and the spring fair and the latest news from London, and Pa relaxed. Now and then he glanced at Cissy with a puzzled frown and a grim quirk of his mouth.

Cissy had twisted the long shawl to hang down her front until she looked like a walking pile of bedding. Look dumb as a booby bird, she told herself. Move slow as a hog in a pease patch. Should he speak, be peevish.

She loitered in the center of the room, arms hanging at her side, staring at the floor. From under her lashes she met Master Bunyan's eyes and thought he tried not to laugh.

Pa called out the window to Frank who was chopping wood and ordered him to escort the gentlemen to see the cells. Then he made an excuse to hand Cissy an empty pitcher to fill. "Are you daft? Sick? Make up to Master Cobb or I'll wring your nose by and by!"

Cissy clawed her bare arms, raising wheals. "Oh I am sick! I'd best take to my bed for a while, Pa."

Since the visitors were now out of sight, he twisted her arm until she bit her lips together for pain. "You simpleton! I'm not fooled by your antics! Don't be playing mouse-shy anymore or you'll pay for it when they're gone! Ask Master Cobb to take you to the fair come spring. And remember what I told you in the pantry."

We be as good as dead, she thought dully, lifting her head and abandoning her play-acting. Only I can save us.

"That's better." Pa was still glaring at her. "Follow after Master Cobb now and ask him prettily."

Cissy went downstairs, but before she could speak, Paul Cobb pulled her aside angrily and showed her a paper. Apparently her charade had not been wasted. He knew she didn't care for him. "Look at this list of names to be sent to the king for pardon. Look especially at number four," he said. "Do you see Master Bunyan's name on the list?"

Cissy read down the column of names. They were in alphabetical order. "No."

"His name was number four, but I've blotted it out so it will never be read. He will rot in Bedford Jail. I mind how you favor him, and no doubt he speaks against me for being a true Churchman. I never liked him. I mind how you put me off, Mistress Nidd, but I'll have my way. Look at me!"

His mean little eyes glittered, and she was forced to face him. "That's only the beginning of what I can do!"

Black St. Bartholomew's Day

The next month Gil's first letter came from Holland. Frank gave it to her when she took him a jug of water in the field. Hiding the letter under her apron, Cissy made an excuse to go to her room. Pa was collecting tolls while the boys were busy plowing. Eagerly she opened his letter.

Dearest Cissy,

My happiness rises and falls on whether I will hear from you. I am safe and working. There be fine books on architecture here and much to see. Write and tell me everything you do, everything you think.

There was more, describing the strange houses the Dutch lived in, but Cissy kept only the personal parts in her mind. She answered immediately, dipping a quill pen into a pot of ink and writing swiftly across the heavy paper. Pa was always particular to have nice writing material in the house for his monthly reports on the jail.

Gil,

Gil Turpin, yes, I will write volumes. I love you truly, I'm waiting, don't be long. Do you really want to know all about the spring planting? I have my little garden of flowers in a sunny spot. I love their faces. I can imagine them pushing down feet and poking out root-toes. I heard tell once that plants breathe, isn't that queer? And I keep the grass trimmed. After rain the smell is so good. The grass drinks it down, the roots sip. . . . Oh, Gil my love, none of this means anything without you here. Only words, words, to fill pages lest I go mad. I send this off at once and will write again tomorrow.

All my heart's love,
Cissy

She folded and sealed the letter with wax, wrote his first name only on it, and ran back out to the field. Seeing that Harold was napping under a tree, she sat a little way off with Frank.

"Answered already?" He grinned and hid the letter in his shirt.

"When will it be picked up?"

He shook his head. "I never know. Cissy, you couldn't have chosen a nobler fellow, though he be a highwayman."

She smiled in agreement. "He is my true love, and not another."

Back out in the yard she began some garden work to keep from missing Gil. With her back to the jail, she knelt by a lilac bush and flicked up dirt with a hand shovel to plant lettuce. Pa was on the bridge, involved in a long conversation with a horseman delivering newspapers from London. Dull reading, they were usually a month late.

She patted the lettuce seed into the ground. This way no one would suspect that underneath was a small metal box with money inside that she'd taken from Pa's bag of true coins. Before he even had time to count the money from Coronation Day, she'd stolen a handful of gold coins for her dowry.

"A new queen we'll have," she heard the horseman shout. "Catherine of Portugal will sail up the River Thames in London in a gold barge. And a thousand other boats will be on hand to welcome the new bride of King Charles."

Cissy fluffed a little soft earth over the lettuce seed. Lettuce liked shade. So did cabbage, and she planted four rows.

She loved summer, and it would be here in no time. Every day something different in the garden ripened for eating. The trees hung heavy with fruit. She would work hard and write Gil, and time would fly by like the cherry-breasted birds that skipped on the branches overhead.

Dear Gil, my very dearest Gil,

I have a whole candle for myself, and Pa and Harold are out to a town meeting. Frank is asleep by the fire. I'm in my little bedroom in the wall; it's as snug as a thimble. Summertime is fair time, with all the country people coming into Bedford with corn and sheep for sale. If only you could be here to take me to the fair.

What did I do today? Same as I did aforehand. Sliced near a bushel of tomatoes and layered them on the wooden trays; put them out to dry in the sun; brought them in at night. Then I'll string them on a cord and hang them in the attic. I'll learn everything I can to be a thrifty housewife.

And apples, she thought. Apples to slice and dry and string on a cord. Onions to braid up by their tails and hang in the sun.

The attic must be filled with dried food, and the cellar with turnips and potatoes against the winter. Cissy picked up her pen.

Gil, I must tell you that I read from a real Bible bought from Master Bunyan. It be all inspired by God Himself, says Master Bunyan. I can read chapter after chapter, not just bits and pieces picked out by someone else.

The Bible explains how Jesus is the everlasting Son come down to earth to die in our place. He was a real man and worked with His hands, like you want to, Gil. He built things of wood, like you long to build.

She raced on in her enthusiasm.

Gil, dear, maybe you would like to read about Him, too. Can you get a Bible in Holland? My dear, this Book tells how Jesus has all power and can answer prayer.

She stopped again. She still only read prayers from the Prayer Book, but it occurred to her that if only she knew the Lord Jesus for herself, she would ask Him to help her and Gil.

Two lawbreakers ask for help? She shook her head sadly. No, there must be some kind of punishment to suffer first, before she dared to ask for anything.

But Jesus seemed real to her. The Jesus of the Bible almost seemed to call to her out of the pages as she read. She wouldn't be surprised if some night He said, "Cissy Nidd, follow Me, and I will make you into a real Christian."

A few mornings later, Cissy walked into town and took Betsy Bunyan some spinach and scallions from the garden. Betsy was busy bathing the children, so Cissy didn't linger.

She stopped at the baker's and bought six hot loaves. When she reached home, Pa handed her the *London Weekly Courant*. "Where have you been dawdling so long? Take this to Master

Bunyan; 'twill interest him mightily. Ask him to come up tonight for another game of chess.''

Cissy read the headlines as she walked: more about the new queen; a crude drawing of the latest petticoat to be worn with ball gowns. In smaller print at the bottom of the page: ''The Act of Uniformity became law this past May 19th.''

Cissy offered Master Bunyan the paper and leaned against the doorway. ''Pa asks you to come up and play chess tonight.''

''Pleased I am, yes.''

''Be you interested in the new queen or the latest fashions?''

''Neither. I see the Act of Uniformity is now the law. Such villainous things be often served up in ordinary words.''

''What does it mean?''

''It means that all clergymen must consent to using just the *Book of Common Prayer* in worship, or lose all. House, money, furniture, even the clothes from their backs. And all clergymen of England must be ordained over again as Anglicans.''

Cissy couldn't understand his concern. ''You are not an official clergyman, and you are quite safe here with us.''

''I'm not worrying one mite about myself. This article says two thousand clergymen are expected to rebel at the act! There will be bloodshed all across England.''

''Two thousand?''

''Yes, and I would guess there are about fifteen in our own county who would not consent to this outrage. Many now want to be able to read and preach direct from the Holy Scriptures. Cissy, have you been reading the Holy Scriptures?''

She nodded.

''And have you not felt God's call?''

She shook her head. Could she ever tell him of her love for a highwayman and her part in passing false coin? Yet she *must;* she felt now she must tell someone.

Master Bunyan laid the newspaper aside. ''My thanks to your father. I'll read it later and return it so he can loan it to another.

Cissy, I fear for your soul. Poor girl, a struggle is written all across your face. You are passing through a time of despair, same as I did. Will you not trust me to advise you?''

Helpless tears filled her eyes, and she couldn't lift her head to look at him.

"Cissy, I trust you, else I would not tell you this. The believers of Bedford can no more meet openly for fear of arrest. Not even as few as three can meet, though it be lawful. Do you know of Wain Wood at Preston?''

"Yes.''

"I sometimes preach there in the dead of night in a hollow with sentries posted around. Hundreds of Dissenting Christians gather. But there's a closer place in the Holmes Wood, at the reedy inlet of the Ouse, only five miles away.''

Cissy showed her surprise. "Does Pa know?''

"The cell door is sometimes left open, you know that. Who plays as good a game of chess as I? Your pa has been most lenient, but from now on, I'm afraid things will change. The new men in Parliament vow to stamp out all Dissenters from the realm. Dissenters in other countries have had their ears slit, heavy fines laid upon them, and a few I know were actually hung!''

Cissy only half-listened, such was her own unhappiness.

Master Bunyan went on, "Cissy, poor soul, will you go with Betsy some night? The two of you can ride on Master Fenne's horse. His good wife will mind my children.''

"I'd be so feared! What if they miss me here?'' Cissy whispered.

"Trust God as we all do.''

"Do you never visit Betsy when you're out?''

"Never. I wouldn't danger her so. I see her when she visits the jail, and that must be enough.''

"Mayhap I'll go sometime.'' She shivered at the very notion.

August passed while Cissy worked out a new lace pattern for the fair. All the women put their best lace forward to sell. Others sold aprons or jam, brooms or pigs. There would be a pie-eating contest and an auction.

This year, the biggest fair ever would be held in Bedford on St. Bartholomew's Day. That morning of August 24th showed pink and crimson at dawn, but by seven o'clock the sky was blue, smooth as a robin's egg. The air was hot already, and Cissy felt she was wading in light; the sun was that obliging.

The fair was to be held at St. Peter's Green on the far side of town. By eight o'clock, Cissy could see carts and villagers crossing the River Ouse, coming in from all the hamlets and hollows, laden with flowers, food, and crafts.

At noon Cissy dressed herself in her new blue gown. Pa had bought it for her, but she wasn't deceived. "I'm the bait in the trap," she told Tabby. She fastened a bunch of pink snapdragons in her dark red hair, which hung in loose curls.

Yes, she had agreed to walk at the fair with Paul Cobb, but it was only for show. What harm could it do? No banns had been read in church so far, and her father was silent on the subject. She whispered again to Tabby, "Pa has been 'most meek lately, not forcing my hand to marry. He needs me for the garden work, I suspect."

Cissy tried to reassure herself. Master Cobb was coming to fetch her in a coach; he would buy her anything she fancied; she would have a good time and stay late. At sundown it would all end. She'd never agree to see him again, and she'd write Gil a most humorous account of the fair.

"Good morning, fair!" she sang softly. Then she added to herself, "Don't think beyond today; have a wonderful time, my girl, for you've never before been allowed to stay out 'til dark."

Paul Cobb's coach arrived after dinner, and he seemed relieved to find her smiling. "Cissy, my dear, you are stunning in blue!" He kissed her hand and helped her into the coach, managing to step on one of her slippers and crush the edge of it.

Master Cobb was booted and spurred, a vain demonstration, for he had not been able to ride in years. Green garters with

79

tassels dangled from his fat knees, and he wore all shades of green. He looks like a green horse, Cissy thought, ready for pasture.

Five long blocks they rode, and several times the coach's wheels stuck in a pothole of the road, nearly tipping over. The clay roads of Bedford were crowded with people hurrying to the fair. How they stared to see the jailer's daughter riding in a coach.

"Look your fill!" Cissy cried soundlessly, turning up her nose. "I could marry a townsman, I could, but my heart is given to an architect!"

Once on St. Peter's Green, Cissy looked around in delight. The fair was almost as exciting as London. Four wandering minstrels playing violins stopped before them.

"Does milady like a tune?"

"Oh, yes. Can you sing 'Come Shepherds, Deck Your Herds'?"

The minstrels began to sing and play, then the youngest held out a hollowed-out, long-handled gourd, and Master Cobb dropped in some money. "Sing 'As at Noon Dulcina Rested,' " he ordered.

When it was over, he took Cissy's arm. "Come, my Dulcina; let us view the pie eating."

Two men stood in a ring of people, devouring pies as fast as a woman handed them up. Nearby, other young men wrestled and bowled ninepins, loud and rowdy. Apple pies were being sold, hot out of the oven. Cissy pointed to some bonbons, and Master Cobb paid for a paperful. Then he bought her a brass box with a Paris emblem on it.

"The townsmen are a little worried about the outcome of this fair," he confided to her. "The constable has extra men standing about. The long-standing feud between the butcher and the weaver may come to a head today."

A tinker passed them, singing:

"Have you any work for a tinker?

Any old bellows to mend?
Brass pots, iron pots,
Skillets or frying pans?''

He carried his anvil on his back and his tools of pliers, snippers, and soldering iron in a basket.

"Shall we look at the pillory?" Paul Cobb asked.

Cissy shook her head vigorously. Master William Perks had been put in the stocks this day, and he would be pelted with rotten eggs because he'd sold sugar with sand mixed into it.

Young men and single women strolled through the fair, wearing the emblem of their craft on their sleeves, offering to sell their services for a year. I'll never have to peddle myself like that, thought Cissy, for I'm promised to an architect!

The afternoon hours melted away as they watched races and listened to folk singing. When they stopped by the lace table, an old woman with a face like a dried apple presented Cissy with a blue-ribbon prize. Master Cobb beamed, and Cissy clapped her hands for joy.

"Another prize for design!" she said. "It's my own pattern, and if I prick it out on paper and send it to the printer, I'll earn a shilling!" All the sights and noises and smells of the fair—she was storing them in her mind for Gil. She pretended he was by her side instead of Paul.

"I'll give you a gold guinea to sit in my garden and sew," Master Cobb said, squeezing her arm.

They turned in the direction of a sudden loud quarrel. Through an unfortunate mistake, the butcher and the woolen weaver had been allotted spaces side by side. The weaver was trying to demonstrate his craft, but the butcher, who earned money by cutting the throats of pigs he sold, had splashed the blood onto the weaver's loom. A dozen rough fellows took sides, shouting to the weaver to defend himself.

The butcher taunted the weaver with choice insults. "You offspring of a rotten squash!"

"You, that can't afford salt for your cabbage!" the weaver screamed back.

The sun leaned into the west, and Master Cobb said, "Walk toward my coach, for I see trouble brewing, and we don't want to be caught in it. Will you have some supper at yonder booth first?"

"I am hungry," Cissy admitted. "Look! What's that parade coming down the Stevington Road?"

To the north they saw a crowd of men on foot, with men on horseback driving them on. Master Cobb tightened his hold on her arm. "No parade. They're bringing prisoners, Dissenters that they caught in a secret meeting. Too many for little Bedford Jail, though!"

Dissenters caught in the woods near Stevington! Then Master Bunyan had been caught preaching to them! Cissy pulled away from her escort and scrambled up onto a bench to see better. "There be forty—no, fifty—sixty, mostly men."

A cabbage stalk sailed by, just missing her face, and Master Cobb tried to lift her down. Stones and bricks flew through the air. Cissy jumped up nimbly to a higher perch. The prisoners were marched right down to St. Peter's Green and ordered to stand in rows.

"Traitors! Traitors to the Crown!" shouted a farm boy, throwing a stone.

"Traitors!" Others took up the cry, pushing closer to the men. At the same time the weaver's patience evaporated, and just as Cissy looked down, he left his loom and with a mighty lurch kicked over the butcher's table.

"Hi! Hi-ho! A fight!" The out-of-town roughs surged toward the weaver and the butcher. The Bedford youths, inflamed by the sight of adults fighting, joined in the uproar.

"Master Fenne, the hatter! He is a Dissenter! Break down his door and stomp on the hats!" cried one boy. Other young men began to call out names, though most townspeople knew who the Dissenters were.

"Thomas Cooper, the heel maker! Widow Tilney! Thomas Arthur, the pipe maker!"

A band of men dashed away from the Green on horseback. So swiftly did they work that in a short time the horses pulled back carts loaded with Dissenters' household goods to be auctioned off to the angry crowd. So thoroughly was the Widow Tilney's home plundered that Cissy recognized bedsheets and dishes and irons from the fireplace, even drapery torn down from the bed's canopy.

Fired-up men ran to even old scores—to pull Dissenters' gates off their hinges; to turn chickens and pigs loose; to let cows out of barns. Roughs from out of town broke into the closest churches and began to ring the bells.

"Stop them!" Cissy screamed down to Master Cobb from where she stood above it all. "Make them stop! They will listen to you!"

"The Dissenters be lawbreakers," he growled. "Come down; I'm feared for your safety. These fools are half-mad. For shame on you, to climb about like a wild girl with folk looking on."

"They be our neighbors!" Her foot slipped and she would have toppled face down, but Master Cobb caught her.

"I see the constable! He's standing there, approving it all!"

Paul kept his arm around her. "Cissy, love, I thought perhaps Christmas would be the time to wed. We'll have a beautiful ceremony here in St. Paul's, naturally, then a wedding supper for, say, two hundred. . . ."

Cissy struggled to free herself, still staring at the crowd. "There's a cart with an anvil and shovels—it must be poor Isaac the blacksmith's. How will he live?" she cried. "There's three cartloads of new wood! I know it belongs to Master Cooper. The wood is worth more to him than his cobbler's bench, for he has little enough!"

She blinked back tears. "Master Cobb, pray stop them! Oh, poor Widow Tilney, she that gave me the bobbins I use! You must stop them!"

"Cissy, calm your nerves, love, and come away. You shall address the invitations with your own hand, and you shall choose the desserts."

"Let me go, Paul Cobb! I hate you!"

His strong hand gripped her arm like a shackle. "Run to the coach! Hurry! Let me go first and do you follow close; the mob is going mad. We are in danger. Hurry!"

The coachman saw them and fought his way to their aid, cracking his whip over the heads of people. "Slash them!" Master Cobb ordered, and the coachman lashed his whip down across shoulders.

The crowd screamed in rage, but it parted to let Cissy and Master Cobb through. Two of his friends appeared out of nowhere. The four of them clambered into the coach, and Cissy heard the wheels spin and grind. The coach jerked, picked up speed, and rumbled away from the Green.

"Oh! My new dress is torn! Oh, Master Cobb, what will happen to the poor—" She looked around, confused. "But who are these other two gentlemen?"

Master Cobb didn't answer; he leaned out the window and bawled to the driver, "To my house, Dick!"

"No, no, take me home!" Cissy wrenched the door open and would have thrown herself out, but one of Master Cobb's friends held her fast and covered her mouth with his hand.

"I only want to show you my beautiful home. It will soon be *your* home." His mouth touched her ear. "Just to peep in the windows, lovey, and you'll change your mind about becoming Mistress Cobb. Why only think, you can exchange your jail house home for my lovely place."

Cissy couldn't move, wedged between him and one of the strangers. The other man sat facing her, holding a lap robe. He could throw it over my head and smother my cries, Cissy thought, if I fight them.

The coach bumped all the way down Long Street, turned, and stopped outside Master Cobb's country estate. Cissy was cold with fear. She knew very well that he intended to ruin her reputation, to make it look as though she wanted to stay with him that night. Her lips couldn't form the words, but silently she cried, "Master Bunyan's God—save me!"

"Cissy, will you be quiet and just go admire the windows of my house, like a lady? No one can hear you anyway, what with all the hubbub." Paul Cobb stepped out of the coach first; Cissy heard a thud, and the big man suddenly clumped down in a heap. She saw that Frank was grappling with Master Cobb's friends, his face ugly with anger.

"Cissy, I feared he'd bring you here," her brother panted. "I kept an eye out for you all day and borrowed Will's horse to follow you. This be the same as kidnapping of you! It won't do for folk to know you were alone after dark with these three!"

The third man pulled a pistol from his waistcoat, but Frank kicked it flying. "Attempted assault, beside," Frank shouted. "Threaten me with a deadly weapon, will you?"

The gentleman stooped to aid Paul Cobb, who had struggled to his knees and was wiping blood from his mouth.

"Run, Cissy, run!" Without a word she took her brother's hand and together they ran in the fading sun glow, down the deserted streets of Bedford, while far behind them the revelry of Black St. Batholomew's Day assailed their ears.

To Be a Pilgrim

Rain, endless rain had marked the autumn months. Cissy didn't enjoy Christmas at all. The joy was gone, as the people of Bedford lived in suspicion of spies and anarchists among them.

Cissy hugged the fireside each night to catch some warmth before she ran up to her cold room. She pitied the two thousand clergymen who had been turned out of their churches on the black day of St. Bartholomew. They found work with pick and shovel if they were able, or they lived off charity.

"What shall their children do? Shall they starve?" Cissy hardly realized she was thinking it out loud.

Pa bent over the table in the kitchen, working on the coins. "Are you still going on about that? Yes, let them starve, as long as the fathers be rebels. I believe I've got this design to match the profile of Charles II. Look, Harold! The laurel wreath is the same. The shield of arms, the cross. Come look at this, Frank."

Cissy looked at Pa blankly. "The whole town is divided— friends against each other. Master Garret reported he saw a Dissenter pray in the woods, and he got a fat reward. Families spy upon families."

"Clergymen are starving to death," said Frank, looking cross, as if he were not interested in the coins any longer.

Could he be feeling the same as I? Cissy wondered.

Paul Cobb had not spoken to her after the day of the fair. Pa hadn't mentioned it, either. Yes, and the deed was the same as kidnapping, she thought. Mayhap they be afraid I'd testify against them. And I would!

Harold melted down a speck of gold small as a pinhead and dipped a brass coin into it. That's like me, Cissy thought. And like Pa. Dipped into religion enough to make the outside look good, but with a false heart. True believers should be like the solid gold coins glowing on the table.

False coin, true coin. False coin, true coin. She said good night and climbed the steps into her cold room. False coin, true coin. Which was she? But she knew, didn't she?

She woke early the next morning and wrote to Gil, though she had received no letter since last month.

Dear Gil,

This is the most dreary time of the year. I miss you so, oh, how I miss you! There is nothing much to do but make lace and do my everyday chores. Come for me soon, Gil, I beg you.

—Cissy

She stood and looked out of the narrow window slit, toward the River Ouse and the water wheel. The meadow beyond still showed green under a light layer of snow, though the lilies had died long ago. The weather was nippy and rain was in the air.

"You, Cissy-y-y!"

She gave up staring at the water wheel and followed the direction of her father's voice to the pantry. "Listen!" He put his ear to the door leading down to the back yard. "Do you hear the flute again?"

Cissy plainly heard the thin piping notes of a flute being played in Master Bunyan's cell.

"Tell him he must hand over the flute. Prisoners are not here to make music."

Master Bunyan had been moved to a cell no bigger than a barrel, its massive oak door banded by iron bolts. He was not even to look out of the peephole.

When Cissy unlocked the door and swung it aside, Master Bunyan was sitting on his three-legged stool reading the Bible. He was very thin, and he wore the grey, strained face of a prisoner.

"Pa wants the flute." She was so ashamed of Pa's pettiness, she couldn't look him in the face.

Master Bunyan stood up and bowed. "Happy I am to see a human being, Cissy Nidd. Betsy has not been to visit for two weeks, four days, and three hours. The children take sick one after another in the winter. If you find the flute, Cissy, you may have it."

Cissy looked around. There was nothing to see save the stool, a low table, a pile of straw for bedding, the rosebush in a pot, an hourglass, and some manuscripts. Master Bunyan shook out his pockets and patted his breeches and jacket. "Not here."

"It's under the straw." Cissy felt mean about plaguing him, but another prisoner had complained to her father about hearing a flute. Master Bunyan obligingly kicked the grubby straw to pieces and the dust flew up her nose and made her eyes water. Wherever had he hidden that flute?

"I'll tell you, Cissy, since I've had a good time teasing your father. I won't play it again, but I won't give it up either. I made it for my boys."

He unfastened one leg of the stool and showed her how he'd hollowed it out. Using the candle flame, he had taken hours to burn out small holes along its side.

"Your father has been fair baffled," he said. "Every time he ran down to claim the flute, I just fastened the leg back on the stool. Cissy, what is troubling you? You don't even smile at my foolery.''

"Nothing." She jangled the keys and made as if to close the door.

"Wait—don't go! See the alphabet blocks I've carved so the boys can learn their letters? Cissy, listen; please listen to me a while. The days are so long and the nights so cold; it helps to talk to a person.

"I'm going to be hung, I know it. I'm only afraid I will falter and show a pale face going up to the scaffold, and men will mock my faith because of it. Ah, Cissy, if you only knew my Jesus, who helps me be content in this dark place!''

Cissy listened. The candle flickered, burning low, and when it went out, the damp, black night of the dungeon would creep up around Master Bunyan, for he had no more candles. Often this winter she'd heard him weeping and trying to stifle the sound. She'd seen him lying on the straw with his coat over his head— weeping, weeping.

This be the saddest time of my life, she thought, for surely naught worse could happen to a person.

"Cissy, are you reading the Bible? Do you know how wondrous a thing it is to read a book? When my first wife and I wed, we had not a spoon nor a dish for the table, but we had two books. Oh, the happiness of those days! I'd rather have the Bible than all the libraries of the universities!''

The dreary air of the cell, the unwashed smell of Master Bunyan, and her mournful thoughts all combined to nudge Cissy away. She heard only parts of what Master Bunyan said.

"Cissy, I dreamed a dream last night—a man in rags with a heavy burden on his back—yet he had a Book to guide him to the Celestial City. Perhaps I'll write it down as a story. Cissy? Poor girl, I'm afeared for you.''

"I must go!''

"Cissy, do you know what a pilgrim is?''

"N-no.''

"A believer in Christ who knows this world is not his home. We're pilgrims and strangers here says the Bible. A pilgrim follows Jesus, Cissy. A pilgrim leaves all behind and sets his eyes upon heaven. Cissy—remember . . ."

"Goodbye, Master Bunyan." Cissy fled upstairs, for she could hardly bear the churning thoughts he stirred in her mind. She almost wished she'd never known him.

"You, Cissy! Bring me the flute!" Pa sat with his stocking feet on the hearth reading the newspaper. "Throw it in the fire," he said.

"I couldn't find it."

Her father crumpled the newspaper, in a temper. "You be lazier every day." He gave her a sharp look. "Hmmm, I see they nabbed him at last." He held up the paper. "Little item here on the last page."

At first, she didn't understand. Who was arrested?

"Swift Nicks himself," chuckled her father but watching her closely. "Arrested as he was crossing back into England. He'll hang for certain."

Cissy knew that her white face gave her away; she saw it in her father's look of delight. She turned without a word and walked out into the open air. "Bring back some watercress for a salad!" her father called, laughing to himself.

Gil, arrested! To be hung! Never to see him! She shivered for a moment in the yard, then walked down the bank and along the river's path toward the water wheel.

The wheel was silent and the miller's house deserted. She turned and looked back at Bedford Jail through the fog. She pictured her father snarling when he found the kitchen door hanging open. She kicked off her wooden clogs. The day was as still as nighttime. A few candles shone in the windows of Swan Inn where the favored people were dining. The cold ground stung her feet, and the damp oozed up through her toes.

There was only one direction to go; for her, one solution to her pain. And here, the river was deep. She couldn't swim; so she would have to wade into the water and hope the strong undertow at that spot would carry her away swiftly.

She thought she heard singing, a man's voice. Often the Dissenters in jail sang to each other. She'd heard them before. Yes, she did hear singing. Master Bunyan's deep bass voice. She hesitated.

> *"Who would true Valour see,*
> *Let him come hither;*
> *One here would Constant be,*
> *Come Wind, come Weather.*
>
> *There's no Discouragement,*
> *Shall make him once Relent,*
> *His first avow'd Intent,*
> *To be a Pilgrim."*

She'd never heard this particular song; he must have just written it. He made songs as easily as she had when a little girl, before her mother died.

A second man's voice took up the tune, and they sang together. The beautiful sound came through the fog that bound her and blinded her and wrapped her like a shroud.

On the chorus, others joined in, their voices cutting through the frosty air. "My right to be a Pilgrim . . . to be a Pilgrim . . . to be a Pilgrim . . . "

Cissy stood still, the words drawing her back from the river. Then Master Bunyan's voice rang out, repeating one of the lines. "*Your* right to be a Pilgrim," he sang. He had changed a word, and Cissy knew he was calling her back. He must have seen the direction she took and guessed her intention. The cold numbed her ankles and crept up her legs, and her bare arms crawled with goose bumps. Why was she standing here in the cold river?

"Your right to be a Pilgrim . . . to be a Pilgrim . . . " When had she ever had any rights? But the words hung over the river, claimed her, drew her home. She ran back to Bedford Jail.

In the yard she realized that her wooden clogs were back by the water wheel, but she left them there. She caught up the ring of jail keys she'd left on the ground. Master Bunyan must have heard them jangle, for he called. "Cissy! Cissy! Step over just a minute. I'll ask the loan of a candle from your father until my wife brings me a pound of them, tomorrow mayhap."

As she reached the cell door, he whispered. "Betsy has been here. Slip out with her tonight at half-past midnight after the watchman cries. She will be by Swan Inn. Go with her to the meeting. Cissy, this time you must go!"

Cissy wiped her eyes with her neckerchief and went upstairs without answering. Her father was still by the fire with his feet on the hearth. He glanced up when he heard her. "Ah, been crying, have you? I thought you'd regret refusing Master Cobb. Looks good to you now, does he? I knew if I said nothing and let you brood over it and pine away, you'd come to your senses."

He threw a log suddenly into the fire and poked it into place with his foot. "He could take a scrawny broom like you and put fine clothes on your back and make you a tolerable-looking woman. Poor wretch, you could have been wed by now and in a fine house and handing out to your old father, who's had the care of you over seventeen years."

He didn't notice her missing clogs. Cissy changed into dry stockings and drank some hot milk to warm her insides.

After supper, when her brothers busied themselves with the coin, she said loudly, "I've had the shivers all day, mayhap a fever; so I'd best take to bed."

Nobody bothered to answer. She curled into a ball under the goose feather quilt and listened for the watchman. Gil . . . no, she dared not even think.

"Ten of the clock, all's well—a cold, foggy night," cried the watchman.

"I'll go to the Dissenters' meeting," she told herself grimly. "This time I must go, or I'll die of my grief."

The watchman passed the bridge. She heard his footsteps go toward Swan Inn. At eleven o'clock the men took to their beds in the next room, and their snores shook the framed needlepoint picture on her wall. At twelve, she stood quietly and pulled a wool shawl over her dress, put a wool cloak on top of that, and wound a warm scarf around her head.

Just as the watchman cried the half-hour, she unbarred the front door and let herself out. She waited until the watchman passed the Inn, then she hurried across the street and looked for Betsy. The fog was thick, dripping moisture like a heavy rain. She could hardly see the road.

Someone reached for her arm and she choked back a shriek, but it was Betsy. "Walk to the edge of this road," Betsy whispered. "Master Fenne is there with horses."

They moved like shadows toward the field and found Master Fenne mounted and holding a horse for them. "Ride behind me," Betsy said, climbing into the saddle. "I turned a corner getting here and came almost eye to nose with the watchman. He didn't see me, though. We'll be back before daybreak. Brother Steven Hawthorne will preach, for your pa dares not let my poor husband out anymore."

They followed the River Ouse north across the meadow. At the entrance to the woods stood a sentry who had sharp ears to hear each horse approaching.

"Welcome, God bless you," he said, as each rider passed by.

The woods were dense, the path partly overgrown in brambles, and Cissy fastened her arms tightly around Betsy's waist lest she jounce off the horse.

Deeper and deeper they rode into the thick growth of trees and bushes. Cissy could barely see the horse and rider in front of them, it was so foggy.

At a reedy inlet of the Ouse they dismounted and stood in a cluster for warmth. Brother Hawthorne was waiting for them up on a rock ledge. Two women stood on each side, holding an apron over his head, since it had begun to drizzle. Cissy recognized the Widow Tilney.

They stood the whole time, since there was no place to sit down. How strange to call this a church, thought Cissy. May God help me tonight, for I have tried everything else.

Brother Hawthorne announced his topic: "The book of Isaiah, chapter thirty-eight and verse seventeen. *For Thou hast cast all my sins behind thy back.*"

Behind God's back? Cissy clung to Betsy and listened intently.

"Hezekiah was sick unto death . . . "

As I am, she thought.

"Instead of peace, he had great bitterness."

Aye, bitterness.

" 'I shall go to the gates of the grave,' said Hezekiah in his despair. He was afraid. Afraid his life would be cut off—chop— as the weaver cuts off thread. He felt that all his bones were crunched up in a lion's mouth; he hurt that badly in his spirit. His eyes were blind from looking upward and seeing no help."

Like me, thought Cissy.

"He grieved, as a dove mourns for a lost mate."

Like me. Gil, Gil, my lost mate.

"Hezekiah had the pining sickness."

This man knows all about me, Cissy thought. Master Bunyan must have told him all my life.

"God says, 'I have seen your tears'!" Brother Hawthorne thundered out. "Dear friends here tonight, He has seen your tears! He knows your dangerous circumstances. Hezekiah's very teeth chattered in fear! He was depressed! But God in love for his soul delivered him!

"My believing friends, who have fled to Jesus for salvation, He has cast all your sins behind His back! Gone! Forgotten! And will He not also deliver us from evil and give us victory during these trying times?"

"Behind God's back," Cissy whispered. "God would put my sins behind His back."

"Let us conclude with a time of prayer. Come to the front of the rock ledge. Goodwives, do you put down a rug for kneeling, kindly."

Cissy never paused nor held back. She walked up to the front of the group with faithful Betsy right beside her. She fell onto her knees next to a praying woman and covered her face with her hands.

"I don't know God," she said, weeping. "I'm afraid of Him."

"Ah, you are coming to God through Jesus, who is all loving," said Sister Fenne, putting her arm around her. "You're coming to Jesus, who so loved you He poured out His soul, an offering for sin. Only trust Him, dear. Forsake sin. Call upon His name; ask Him to save you."

"Kind Jesus, save me, for I give myself to You. Lord, have mercy, it's me, Cissy Nidd. I come to be a pilgrim in this life, to be a true coin, not false coin. Oh, Betsy, I want to confess to you. I want to tell somebody all my sin, but only you."

"I'm here, dear, but you need not tell any soul alive your sin."

No, no, I'm wrong, Cissy thought rapidly. I'd endanger her, and she would feel obliged to report the wicked Nidds.

"Are you sure I may tell only the Lord?"

"Yes, yes, it's in the Book." Sister Fenne held her hand. "Do pray as long as you wish, my dear."

Cissy knelt a while, sobbing and praying in a low tone. All the women fell to crying a little out of sympathy. The men were silent, some praying, some holding the horses, waiting to leave.

Finally Brother Hawthorne spoke. "We must close this meeting and go home before it lightens. The next meeting will be a week from tonight. Do not leave anything behind. Strew the leaves and twigs around so no prints can be seen. Good-bye, and God go with you."

Cissy wiped her eyes and mounted the horse behind Betsy. "Behind God's back! Behind God's back! He can't see them! My sins be gone and my heart is lightsome. I'm not the old Cissy Nidd; I'm somebody newborn all over again."

She hugged Betsy, content to rock and bump over the miles. Just before reaching Swan Inn, she closed her eyes and prayed. "Dear Father in heaven, I'm so new I be not sure I can ask any favor. But if I may ask . . . help me find Gil. Please help me to find Gil Turpin."

The Elephant and Castle

All that week Cissy hunted through the garbage in the wooden box in the kitchen for the newspaper. Finally, she gave up. "Pa never saves the papers," she said to Tabby, lifting her up for a cuddle. "That paper could be miles away by now, passed on by everyone who can't afford to buy."

As week after week went by, the thought of Gil's arrest saddened every lonely hour. "Now I wonder," Cissy said to herself one day; "I wonder if Pa was lying. Every week I read the paper, and there's no notice of a trial for Gil. But neither have there been any letters from him. Yet—how did Pa know that Gil was crossing from Holland to England?"

Week after week, her father reminded her of two important events coming in the spring. First, the banns would be read in the church for her and Paul Cobb. That practically made the union legal. Second, she and Frank would go to London on one last trip to pass false coin and get rid of it all.

Cissy swept the dirt off the back steps with fierce strokes. "And I'll do neither," she told Tabby. "For I will be off afore I commit two such grave sins."

Pa had been almost kind to her, now that his fondest dream was coming closer. Once in a while Paul Cobb came calling, but he was most careful to keep his distance and to speak with exaggerated respect. She saw how the two men winked and smiled when they thought she wasn't looking. "As though I've accepted my fate," she informed the cat.

Still, she must someday tell Pa of her new faith and that she was a Dissenter. The Bible said to witness for Christ.

She had a plan. She'd saved money, stolen money—money robbed from honest people by passing false coin. But mine, she thought rebelliously. I can't give it up, for Pa will never grant me a dowry. He can't afford it, and Master Cobb doesn't need it. So I'll save it against my wedding day and ask Gil what to do.

The metal box of coins was still buried underneath the lilac bush. One evening in May after the sun went down, Cissy dug up the box and replaced it with the smaller but sturdier one Paul Cobb had bought her at the fair. She took out enough for coach fare to London and the four times she must lodge overnight. One of the wives in town had told her the fare and the hour the coach arrived.

The next morning, Cissy ran away. With her Bible and the money tied in a kerchief and only the clothes she wore, she hurried out of Bedford Jail just as the coach was approaching on the North Road. To her relief, no one else got on; the driver cracked his whip and started up. She was on her way to London!

The coach was just a wagon with a cloth hood drawn by eight horses. It could carry twenty people, but only a dozen were inside, none of them from Bedford. A wagoner walked in front, leading the horses.

Five days of travel and four nights bedded down in grimy boarding places used up Cissy's small store of coin. When she finally arrived in London and knocked at Peg Metcalf's door, she was penniless.

The daytime crier, in cocked hat and black gown, ringing a bell, passed her just then. "Wandered away or stolen, a brown horse with a patch of white on right side, carrying a worn saddle. Runaway, a ten-year-old blond boy apprentice, name of Tom, large burn scar on chin."

Mayhap he'll cry me up someday, Cissy thought. I'm under age and Pa could force me back, though I'd like to die first!

A startled Peg opened the front door of The Black Pot. "I'll not pass bad coin again!" Cissy burst out. "So I've run away! I'll work hard, I'll do anything, but I can't live at home anymore!"

Peg made her welcome at once. "Didn't I say you should live here? No need to contact your pa. I always seen how the wind did blow between you two. Our home be your home, such as it is in a Black Pot."

Cissy worked hard, learning quickly, and soon she was at ease in the big kitchen of The Black Pot. The fireplace was three times the size of the one at home, with ovens on each side for baking.

A long wooden table on which to roll pie crusts stood on a flagstone floor. On a spit over the open fire roasted a leg of mutton and a side of beef. Dressed fowl swung overhead.

In the sink, sieves of oysters and deep-sea fish were set to drain. An iron hook suspended the soup kettle over the fire, and Cissy learned the use of skillets, copper pans, and a spice cupboard.

"Cooking for our little Bedford Jail was much simpler," she said to Peg. "Preparing three meals a day in this busy place must give you a backache."

"Sometimes." Peg handed her a small sack of coffee berries to pound. "Use the wooden bowl and rounded hammer. Then brew the mass in boiling water and strain it."

"Do most diners drink coffee?" asked Cissy.

"No, chocolate, the new drink, is all the fashion. It's sold in large chunks. Watch now." Peg grated a lump, poured hot cream over, and served it up in a silver pitcher. "Soothes a stressful stomach, I always tell the diners."

Whenever she thought of Gil, Cissy eased herself with a cup of warm chocolate. Not that it helped much, but she was more hopeful now. Did not God promise to answer prayer? Her prayer was that Gil would come to Christ as Savior. After that . . . well, I will trust God for whatever happens, she told herself.

She learned to set the tables properly, remembering the uses of all nine sizes of pewter dishes. Rabbit was served on long platters, meat pies in deep dishes. The pantry was full of supplies.

One morning, in the lull between meals, Cissy sat with Peg on the front stoop, watching the traffic pass. Jackdaws flew back and forth, landing on the red gabled roofs, chattering and scolding. Cissy bared her arms to the elbows and let the sun warm her.

"Cissy," Peg said abruptly, "we must find you a husband!"

Cissy laughed, but her heart hurt all over again. "Not likely. I'm too busy."

"Cissy, you know I'm fair happy you are here. You are a marvelous help, you are, and I do enjoy playing hostess. Why, you be taking over the job of cook at The Black Pot! We have more business than we can take care of since you came."

Peg fanned her face with a dishtowel and added with a smile, "Why, even Master Pepys of the Royal Navy office took his supper here one night along with his wife. He remarked how I must have hired a cook from Paris!"

Cissy laughed in delight. "Did he say that, really? Oh, it's a happiness to be here and not to be scolded—" She bit off the words.

Peg hugged her. "I do understand. Now the way to find you a husband is to visit a theater where all the young law students go."

"But surely not the ladies?"

"Oh, yes, today they be bold enough. And we'll be bold like them, my girl. Mayhap we'll go only once, then a young dandy will ask to make your acquaintance and come to call. Think, Cissy, a rich husband!"

Cissy turned her head sadly and gazed down the narrow road of the Bridge. Gil. Someday, would he come riding past, his head held high, looking for her? She saw again his narrow face with the deep clefts on either side, his bold eyes.

Then she thought a fearful thing. If he took more note of the London girls—would he change? Would he still love poor Cissy Nidd, jailer's daughter?

Peg chattered on and on. "I won't stand in the way of a good marriage just to hold onto a good cook; no indeed. We'll go to the theater; the latest droll is *Love in a Tub*. 'Tis said to be very funny."

"Dissenters don't approve of the theater." Cissy had explained her decision for Christ one day when they were alone, without telling Peg where the night meetings were held.

"Hush! Don't say that word 'Dissenter,' unless it's softly. You haven't been to Divine Service in months, and it ain't right. You could be troubled by the law."

Cissy rolled her sleeves higher to get the sun. "Look, freckles already. I'm registered in the parish of St. Paul's back in Bedford. They won't notice me in your big church. Why, there be thousands of aliens in London working on shipbuilding and in factories. Frank told me so. Anyhow, I'm just visiting you. I really don't know where to turn next, but the good Lord will guide me."

"Sh-sh, don't speak of the Deity out on the street here; it just isn't done!"

"One night I left my clogs by the water wheel—I told you about that—mayhap Pa has found them by now and thinks I'm drowned. And he wouldn't bother to search. Harold cares naught for me, but I am sorry to put Frank to grief. I doubt that Pa will ever visit London, even though he planned it. The king's edict threatened death for passing false coin."

"And if he does?"

"I'll never go back." Her thoughts swirled uneasily. I'll be of age soon, and Paul Cobb will have no claim on me. He wouldn't want to marry a girl when the whole town must know I ran away from him.

"Oblige me once about the theater," Peg coaxed. "We could shop in Petticoat Lane for new clothes for both of us—well, not new, but almost new. They have very good bargains there. And I need to stop at Master Doctor's for a potion. So, my dear, why don't we close The Black Pot for a day and see London?"

"Oh, I'd like that all right." Cissy ironed her apron down with her hands. Suddenly she turned to Peg. "Could we go to the booksellers' stalls next to St. Paul's?"

"I suppose it could be. What do you want with books?"

"A prisoner back at Bedford writes stories and tracts. I'd like to see if they sell his writings."

"Do you mean Master Bunyan?"

Cissy nodded.

"When I heard him preach years ago, he said, 'No woman should be her husband's slave, though she should not have a brangling-jangling tongue!' "

"What!"

"Indeed he said it! That's the part I remember best."

"I like that!"

Peg clapped her hands like a child. "Let's go today! Trig can put a sign in the window: 'Closed for holiday.' "

"What holiday?"

"*Our* holiday!"

"Let me think a minute." Cissy watched the tilt boats on the Thames, ladies perched in the stern under bright canopies. The boats carried twenty passengers across to shop in London. Boats were faster and more elegant than walking across the Bridge.

"All of Southwark shops in London," Peg said, noting her gaze. "London is a grand seaport. Cargoes from India and China. Foreigners with dark, suntanned skin, some with pigtails, and seamen from all over the world."

The bright pour of the sun on the water lifted Cissy's spirits. Since her conversion in Stevington Woods she had read the Bible morning and night. The old Cissy had, indeed, passed away, with the old fears and guilt. Only one thought disturbed her peace, and she put it down to her overactive imagination.

Behind God's back, she thought. I know He has put my sins behind His back, for He said so. He confirmed it with peace to my soul. But—what if He ever turns around? Will He not see them and be angry? For God is holy, and the holiness of God near breaks my heart. Oh, if only I could find a Dissenter's meeting in London.

Her mind returned to Peg's proposal. Well, she did need another dress. She would wear it to a Dissenter's meeting if she could find one. And she did want to visit the booksellers' stalls.

They closed up The Black Pot and started out on their holiday. Reaching the waterfront, they turned into the East End of London. Peg had been eyeing her, a question written all over her pleasant face. Finally, she spoke. "Cissy, now that you are in a good frame of mind—may I ask? Did your young man go off to the colonies, or was he pressed onto shipboard, or was there another young lady?"

Cissy knew that the hurt in her heart must show in her eyes. "How do you know?"

"I heard you wake in the night and cry in your pillow when you first came to The Black Pot. Night after night, I heard you cry. Day after day, heaving up heavy sighs. Sometimes you'd stand in one spot with your arms in the flour and forget to measure enough for the dough."

"Yes, he's gone." She couldn't bring herself to say more.

"Alas, a pity! Well, if he had to go off, there are others. Don't step in the puddles." She took Cissy's elbow and pulled her closer to the squalid tenement buildings where the shutters hung by one nail. Open doorways led into caves of darkest night. Poor, poor people, Cissy thought, to live out their lives without ever seeing a meadow or a garden.

Peg took note of her gloom. "My, your hair is a crowning glory; such a strange color, like heart's blood." Cissy knew Peg was trying to console her. "You must never cut it or frizz it, my girl."

"No, he—I mean, I like it long. Dear me, are these streets always so noisy?" Cissy had never seen so many little cramped shops wedged together in crooked rows, so many venders almost back-to-back.

"This is the worst of London," Peg said, "but we have to pass through to get to the clothing. There's pickpockets and all kinds of rascals around. Phew! Hold your spice ball over your nose and keep your purse tight."

Venders cried up their roast chestnuts or birds in cages or pickled eels for a penny. Cissy saw a sign in a lodging place: "Only three pennies a night!" Fish shops and dirty coffee houses lined the way. "Full of crimes and plottings, I'm sure," Peg warned. "Don't ever stop here. We'll eat near St. Paul's."

The alleys around Tottenham Square Court Road were the most dismal. Cissy saw a girl her age swoop up a rotten pear from the street, wipe it on her arm, and munch on it.

"Such low life." Peg held up her skirts a trifle. "A good thing we wore clogs. Take care you don't brush against the dirty creatures. One would think they'd be shamed to live like this."

Cissy looked again at the girl with the pear. We're different outside, she thought, but we both have souls; we're both of the human family. Why is she here, and I living in a better place?

All the smells of rotten fish, fried onions, and garbage caught in her stomach and made her feel ill. She buried her nose in her spice ball. Females in greasy dresses bickered with each other in a strange language. A peddler offered them tripe and ox cheek.

"Have we much further to go?"

"Here's Petticoat Lane," Peg replied, turning left at a corner. "Be sure and note if a gown has worn spots or stains, though I can embroider over them."

The narrow lane stretched out before them. On either side, wheelbarrows and carts overflowed with used clothing. Peg rummaged among the clothes hanging on a rack and pounced upon a silver-colored gown trimmed with scarlet threads. "One sleeve is ripped, but think! I'll take both sleeves out and sew in pale green puffy sleeves. With a bit of green at the neck and a lace petticoat showing, you'll seem like the star in the play. Oh, and a big hat loaded with yellow flowers."

"I don't want to go to the theater," Cissy protested weakly.

"Then I can't go, not alone."

Cissy held the gown up against herself. "It *is* a lovely gown." Hardly fit for a Dissenter meeting, though, but . . . oh, if only Gil could see her in it! He'd not look at the London girls!

"You've earned it. Pick out some slippers and a fan and a nice cambric handkerchief to carry. I have some beads you may borrow."

"You could bargain with a gypsy and win thrice over! I can't deny you."

Carrying their bundles, they crossed town, walking slowly and stopping to look at everything. An old man showed his begging badge, authorizing him to collect money for the poorhouse. "Help the sick and dying, milady." Peg gave him a farthing.

Cissy saw what remained of St. Paul's steeple that fell years ago. The spires still stood, but the lovely church had been desecrated. Peddlers showed their wares up and down the aisles. Beggars slept in every available corner. The streets around the church were full of bookstores, music shops, and doctors' offices.

Peg stopped in front of a shop where Dr. Plum, a learned physician, sold "tablets and plasters for sprains and fractures." Inside, they sat on stools while Dr. Plum pulled down Peg's lower eyelids and examined them.

"I heard tell of a four-penny powder that gives one strength, Master Doctor," Peg said. "Oftimes at the end of the day I'm that tired I could sink."

"No pain anywhere? Then you don't need bleeding. I suspect it's nerves; all females have delicate nerves. I recommend these baby frogs. Swallow one to ease your digestion."

Eyeing Cissy appreciatively, he said, "How are you, dear? What will you have? A cure for corns? A glass eye? Ivory teeth? Spectacles?"

"Nothing, thank you."

"Not even something for the toothache? Now I'll give you a piece of advice free. Put a lock of hair in a hollow tree on a moonless night, and as it rots, it will draw the coughs away."

"What's this?" Peg drew herself up tall so she could stare him down. "Sir! You mock us! Hollow tree, indeed! Come, Cissy. Shut your ears to him; the man's a fool!" She left in a huff, her eyebrows drawn up like hooks.

Cissy noticed that all the men in the streets wore shoes and stockings instead of countrified leather boots. Some men carried muffs. Breeches were edged in deep frills with rosettes at the knees. City fashions, she mused. Wouldn't Gil look handsome in such dress?

Bookseller's Row lay in the shadow of St. Paul's. As Cissy poured over the books in the little shop called The Elephant and Castle, her finger touched a familiar name on a binding. *Christian Behavior,* by John Bunyan. The book was nicely bound, covered with a leather strip which folded over and formed a loop for carrying.

"See here, Peg! I've found the book Master Bunyan wrote. Sir, how much is this book?"

"Four pence. That is Master Bunyan's seventh book. Charmed I am to meet you ladies. I am Francis Smith, publisher and seller."

Cissy curtsied, as he was a man of years. He had massive shoulders under his brown jacket, his hose were an astonishing scarlet, and he had a benevolent face.

"Good morrow," Peg said absently, poking at some dusty books with a frown.

"Do you have Master Bunyan's other books?" Cissy asked.

Master Smith laughed ruefully. No one else was in the shop, so he spoke freely. "No, Mistress. I was ill last week, and while I lay abed the shop was raided again. All the books were confiscated by the government. I paid a fine and they'll let me alone for a while. If you return in three months time, there may be other books. I've had to let Master Bunyan's little book *Grace Abounding* go to another printer. I've only the one copy."

Cissy paid for the book and tucked it into her pocket. "Does Master Bunyan ever come here?"

Master Smith didn't reply, just regarded her with his serious eyes. At length he said, "I don't know who you really are."

"Oh, I'm a friend of his!" Cissy said eagerly. "You can trust me."

"And the other lady?"

"She is like an aunt. I live with her."

A drapery in the doorway swayed a little, and Cissy heard a deep voice she would always recognize.

"Cissy Nidd and Peg Metcalf! Send them along in, Francis. Come right in to the back room here, where I work. Mistress Metcalf, we have met before, I believe. I lived but three doors from you on the Bridge."

The back room was piled high with books, and at a table sat Master Bunyan thoughtfully making corrections on a manuscript. He was even thinner than Cissy remembered. His worn clothes hung on his big frame. Though he smiled, his eyes were drawn and weary.

"Peg, how are you? Did you ever take my advice about serving up the stew in little black pots? Well, Cissy! So you didn't drown after all. Your father thinks so, but I won't enlighten him. I told only Frank that I thought you'd gone off. He and Nellie are promised, did you know? The banns were read in church."

Cissy could have hugged him, but she restrained such show of feeling. And darling Nellie for a sister—what an extra scoop of happiness!

"I wonder at God's ways," she said. "They marvel me! Do send Nellie my love. I was needing some counsel and now I have your book and here you are!"

Master Bunyan stood up and offered them chairs. "Sit down, do, and Francis will bring you tea and whatever else he can find."

"Who let you out?"

"Your pa was in a good mood. I let him win twice at chess. This will be my last time. Look at this newspaper. The Conventicle Act takes effect this very month."

Peg reached for the paper and read aloud: "Anyone over sixteen attending a religious meeting other than Anglican will be fined five pounds, or suffer three months' imprisonment. The second offence will result in six months' imprisonment, houses and land forfeit. For the third offence—deportation to the East Indies as a slave."

Cissy's voice told all her disappointment. "Ah, me, I was longing to find a meeting of believers. I feel an aloneness. Such doubts plague me. Even when I read the Bible, my head swells up with questions. Sometimes the old doubts come back."

"He who never doubted, never believed," murmured Master Bunyan.

"I believe God when He said my sins are behind His back; so I know it isn't He who troubles me."

"The Devil will never cease to accuse your conscience, as long as you are in the flesh. You need to know the Scripture teaching on this so you can answer the Devil. Would you go to a Dissenters' meeting, even knowing the new act?"

Peg had been silent, her eyes switching from Master Bunyan to Cissy, but now she twisted her purse in her hands nervously. "Master Bunyan, I appeal to you! Cissy is not used to city life, as you well know. She must not go out alone at night. This isn't a little village like Bedford. This is London!"

"What is 'safe,' good friend?" asked Master Bunyan with a smile. "Could not the Lord stop her breath under the covers at sleep, or while she sups in the house? Does God protect only from dawn to sundown, then cast us aside after six o'clock? Why don't *you* go to a meeting with her? Will you promise not to betray them if I tell you where?"

"Right here, I suppose," said Peg.

"No, too obvious. Poor Francis has enough trouble over getting a license to publish my books, great soul that he is. Do I have your word?"

Peg nodded unwillingly. "My word on it, but it's no promise to attend. Trig would turn me out and bolt the door if I ever thought of such a thing."

"God can make him blind when you go out the door or keep him asleep—or bring him along! Don't be fearful. Do you know where the Bear Inn is, foot of London Bridge in Southwark?"

"Ummm, Bear Inn. I don't often go to Southwark, but I could find it."

"A link boy with a lantern could guide you for a farthing."

Peg hesitated. "I—I just don't know if I could."

"Oh, Peg! Let's go some night!" Cissy exclaimed. "If you would only go with me once, I'd do anything for you. I—I'd go to the—you know what we talked about." It just occurred to Cissy that she was ashamed to have Master Bunyan know she would go to see a play like *Love in a Tub.*

"Let's wait and see. Why, we'd be breaking the law! Arrested! My heart near stops at the very thought!"

"I'm not afraid. God protects Master Bunyan when he goes about."

"As you stand facing the Bear Inn on High Street," he said, "pass six doors to the left. Directly across the street is a chocolate house. In the cheese loft overhead, a handful of Dissenters meet on a Sunday night at nine o'clock.

"The owner is a Dissenter, a man named Hayworth. Engage him in conversation and say to him, *To him that knocks, it shall be opened.* If he still doubts you, say, *Narrow is the way, and few there be that enter.*"

Cissy locked the words in her mind. "How be things in Bedford?"

"The Dissenters no longer keep written minutes of their meetings, they are in such danger. Many Christian brethren are in prison or ruined financially. Many have denied Christ.

"Oh, I do mourn for England and for the sins committed by this government! God will judge this nation! Godlessness everywhere—but all the sinners in Divine Service come to the Lord's Day! I fear what will happen. Something terrible is going to happen!"

Customers entered the shop, and Bunyan fell silent, motioning them to leave. Out on the streets, a boy selling the latest copies of the paper the *Public Intelligence* cried up the headlines, and Cissy's blood turned cold:

TEN THOUSAND DEAD OF PLAGUE
IN AMSTERDAM!
PLAGUE SPREADS TO LONDON!

Behind God's Back

The little link boy waited in the doorway of The Black Pot, his lantern shining marigold yellow against the black drapery of the sky.

Finally—finally—we are going out, thought Cissy. Peg had been weeks deciding, but the time was tonight.

Cissy, lingering in the bedroom by the mirror, listened to Peg and Trig talking, but her mind was on the ruby at her throat. I must keep it hidden, else they ask questions. Mayhap it even be snatched off my neck by some rude oaf. She tried on a scarf, lapping it over her neck and tucking the ends into her collar.

"Step inside, boy, and shut the door behind you," Trig said. "You're letting in the damp. Stand near the fire if you want. Those two spendthrifts in there are primping and decorating themselves with all kinds of newfangled notions. Almost two hours they've been about it. Ah, the folly of it! It's a naughty venture, and I do believe I have an empty noddle to let them have their way."

"And it took all of two months to win you over," said Peg, swirling out from the bedroom, grand as a lady in waiting in her indigo gown of brocade with a gold petticoat. "Boy, how is the fog?"

"Thicker 'n mush, Mistress. I could've supped on it and put some by in my pocket for morning."

"Give him a bite of the leftover cake," Peg said to her husband.

"I thought Cissy was saving it to make us a nice pudding," Trig grumbled as he pinched off a very small piece. "You can't be hungry, boy, are you?"

The boy, thin as a knitting needle, fastened his eyes on the cake. "I hardly mind it anymore. Once when I had a whole apple I took sick of the colic, so it's best not to eat too often."

Cissy made her appearance. When Peg saw her, she spread out her hands in great satisfaction. "Didn't I tell you, Trig? The girl's a beauty! There will be lads a-plenty with eyes for her tonight. A brow like wax. Cheeks that can flush like the sweetbrier rose—that is, if you try, Cissy. You must practice holding your breath to bring the color to your cheeks. Did you chew a few raw poppy seeds with sugar to make your eyes seem larger? So many littles to think of when one goes out to the theater."

Trig snorted. "This be the first and last time you go out. I'll see you across the Bridge, then come back for you at ten o'clock."

"Won't you attend us at the theater?" Peg coaxed.

"No such nonsense for me. Blasted waste of time."

"Silvery grey is your color," Peg continued, turning Cissy around and around to admire the gown. "What do you want with that scarf on?"

"My—my neck is cold."

"Let me show you how it be worn." Peg fussed with the scarf and managed to pull it off. "There. Oh, Cissy! Is that a ruby?"

"A ruby!" Trig narrowed his eyes and crossed the room to see. "A ruby it is! Cozened out of my money, I was. How much did you give for it?"

Cissy's eyes smarted with anger. "I didn't spend your money! The ruby was given to me more than three years ago—by a friend. Peg, I tell you true. I'd scorn to tell a lie."

Peg moved close to Trig and spoke in his ear, but Cissy heard: "There was a young man . . . something happened . . . say no more on it, pray."

The little link boy, who had taken the liberty of creeping closer to the warm fire, had fallen asleep in the chimney nook.

"Wake up, boy!" Trig wrapped himself in his cloak. "What an impudence! D'ye think you are at home?"

Cissy fastened the clasp of the long hooded cloak she'd bought in Petticoat Lane. "Where is your home, boy?"

He jumped to his feet, instantly awake. "Anywhere, long as it don't rain on me. I'm ready, Master, and I know London Bridge and Southwark like I could walk it down-side-up with m'eyes shut."

"Can he sleep by the fire 'til it be time to get us at ten?" Cissy asked.

"No, Mistress, thank'ee." The boy wagged his head sadly. "In two-three hours time I can earn fourpence, maybe more."

"A manly minded lad, knows he must earn a living," Trig growled. "You, boy, be back here before ten."

The link boy led the way across London Bridge, Cissy, Peg, and Trig following. Cissy held hands with Peg, sliding her feet cautiously over the slippery cobbles. The fog welled up from the river, thick and wet, and oozed over their woolen cloaks. Sooty fog that could be tasted.

Cissy held a pomander ball of lavender over her mouth and nose and stayed close to Peg. If Pa could see her now! Or Paul Cobb. Or . . . Gil. No, don't think on it, she told herself; I will find him someday.

Shuffle—shuffle; slip—slip; on they went, following the ray of light from the boy's lantern. Strange, Cissy thought, how Peg now asked the loan of her Bible every Saturday morning when

Trig went fishing. How good it made her feel. For the first time in her life she had a friend.

The link boy stopped in front of the theater, and Cissy saw four tall white columns supporting a fancy balcony with many windows, tapers in all of them. Lanterns shone across the downstairs porch and onto the steps.

"I'll be back at ten or after with the boy," said Trig. "Now mind you, behave as ladies and meet me right at this door. Several of my old merchant friends may be here tonight, so they'll see no harm comes to you."

He and the link boy turned back toward the Bridge. Cissy stood on the porch and watched the boy's light fade away to a golden pinpoint.

"Don't go in yet. Let me think." Peg held her back. "Anybody knowing Trig will tell him we left when the play was half over. Are you really set upon going to the other place? I'll live out my days not knowing how the play ends."

"Yes, yes; you promised, Peg. We made a bargain—but oh, now I don't feel right about it. I don't care for the play at all. Who knows what things we might see that would offend us? Oh, my heart longs after the meeting." Cissy stared into the theater. "How noisy and brawling it sounds in there. What will the Dissenters think of my hair? You've got ringlets pasted all over my forehead. I won't dare to take the cloak off, not with the fancy dress."

"Dearie me, dearie me, let me think! We'll say we felt faint halfway through. . . . "

"I'm sure we will—the noise in there! Oh!" Cissy ducked as a rotten apple was thrown out the door and missed her head. "We found a link boy and went for a cup of hot chocolate—"

"Two women alone on the streets?" Peg exclaimed. "Trig's friends would think ill of us."

"But no one will recognize us in this fog," Cissy pleaded.

"Oh, dearie me!" Peg wrung her hands. "Well, let's trust in God to get us to the cheese loft! I read something in your Bible the other day—Oh dear, here comes a coach full of gentlemen. Go ahead in, Cissy. We can't stand here like a pair of bold faces. Have your penny ready for the man with the collection box.''

A troop of young men wearing rich brocade coats and beaver hats piled out of the coach. Cissy turned to look, saw one man stand apart to clean his boots, saw a skulking, hunched-over shadow approach out of the fog with a raised club.

"Sir, beware!" she screamed. "Behind you! Behind you!"

He whirled, sidestepped, and the blow fell instead on the coach fender. The coachman hurried down from his perch to survey the damage.

The young man she had warned bounded up the steps to the porch. He was a handsome dandy with slightly bulging eyes and brown hair falling down to his shoulders. His blue outfit was tied with a wide silk sash hanging down in fringes.

He bowed over Cissy's hand. "Mistress, I thank you with all my heart. 'Twould be a sad thing to have my skull split on this evening, for I have put some of my own money behind the production of this play. I am grateful for your quickness, Mistress— um, Mistress—"

"I am Mistress Metcalf of The Black Pot, Master Pepys," Peg answered for her. "We have had the honor of serving you supper a few times. This is my niece, Cissy Nidd. Cissy, dear, Master Pepys is a clerk of the Royal Navy."

Cissy curtsied beautifully; she knew it. "I'm pleased I could be of help," she said modestly.

"Ladies, are you alone? I beg you honor me by sitting in a balcony stall with me."

Cissy made her decision. "Thank you kindly, sir, but we are not alone." Was not God with them? "In faith, we be but passing and shall meet our friends further on." She pushed against Peg a little to make her move.

He raised bushy eyebrows. "Not attending the theater?"

"No!" Cissy almost laughed to see Peg's dismay. "But I thank you again, sir; we are both much obliged for the offer."

Master Pepys smiled, as if reluctant to let them go. "Mistress Nidd, I owe you my life, I do believe! I'll not forget your quick warning; on my honor I won't."

Inside a fiddler began to scratch away; so all the gentlemen bowed and left them. "Walk toward the chocolate shop," Cissy said. "You know where it is, don't you? We be early, but we'll sit and talk. I'd never feel right about that sort of company, Peg, and I was wrong to make such a poor bargain with you. Will you forgive me and come to the meeting anyhow?"

Peg sighed. "Yes, dear, though Trig will never again let me out after he hears of our goings-on and how we never got to the play."

"We'll tell the truth, without revealing the cheese loft."

"Oh, dearie me, dearie me." Peg fell to lamenting again. "What will my man say? Turn left here, Cissy; it be further on."

"No, Master Bunyan said go toward Bear Inn."

"I don't know . . ."

"Oh, Peg, now I'm not sure."

They held hands and turned in circles. "Link boy! Is there a link boy?" called Peg. "We should have asked the gentleman to fetch us a link boy."

The fog was so thick Cissy felt the coughs coming on. She coughed until her eyes streamed and her throat was raw.

"Muffle your cough, do," urged Peg. "We can be found by the wrong sort of person if you be so noisy."

Just at that moment they bumped into a tall man in a wet coat and a hand closed on her arm. He swung a lantern light over her face. Cissy drew in breath to scream, but he set the lantern down on the paving and put his arms around her.

"Cissy Nidd! Cissy, I can't believe this! You, in London! You, out alone on the street, and in this dangerous place. And in such costume—not even covered up! Oh, my little love, what terrible thing has happened? Cissy, are you hurt?"

"Gil!" Cissy reached her hands up to his face. "Oh, Gil Turpin, my love."

"Who is this? Sir, who be you? Take your hands from my niece, I say, or I shall rouse this town with screams!" Peg sounded terrified.

"Shhh, Peg, this is the one—the one who gave me the ruby."

Peg was silent, and Cissy saw her staring at them both in horror. "I know you from somewhere. I can't recollect—yet I know you. I know your voice."

"You are mistaken," Gil said abruptly. "We are both from Bedford. Cissy, come with me—now—to France. Holland is full of plague, and they say it be here in London already. The authorities hush it up. I'll take your female companion home safe, but leave everything and come with me. Tonight!"

"Wait, Gil, my dear. Wait. I must tell you. I am a Dissenter—"

"Is this my Cissy Nidd?" he demanded in a shocked voice. "This is no time to talk about religion. Don't you understand what I'm saying about the plague? Has your love died, then, that you prefer city life?"

Peg spoke up firmly. "Sir, we cannot remain here in the street quarreling like low-class folk. Pray, come into the chocolate shop. I know you now, sir," she went on and looked at him meaningfully.

"Well, then you know I cannot come into the chocolate shop or any other public place. And I've told you about the plague being in London; so come away with us and welcome. And Cissy here, will vouch for my honor."

"Do you love this man?" Peg intoned, sounding so much like a marriage ceremony in church that Cissy had to laugh.

"Indeed, and in truth and before God, I love this man. Gil, hear me out. I have followed Jesus and put my faith in Him—not the creeds of the church—but in a personal Savior. I cannot wed you yet, because—"

"Give me no *becauses*." He shook her a little. "I've had a deal of trouble finding you and near thought I'd die when your Pa said you drowned."

"He said you were caught re-entering England."

"He lied! We be no longer friends, and he will do me harm if he can." Gil's hand tightened on her arm. "Cissy, I hoped you'd seek refuge with Peg; so I risked my life to come to London. Trig told me where you'd gone. Oh, the shame of it, to find you wandering the street at night!" Before she could explain, he bent low and whispered, "I did talk to Master Bunyan. He tried to help me, my little love. He did point me to your Savior. But I cannot. I'd have to repay. . . . I'd have to surrender to the Crown. Do you know what you're saying? Then what would happen to the two of us?"

"Gil, God answers prayer. Do give Him time." She hid her face in his shoulder and began to cry. "Write to me! Oh, don't leave me again without letters! I'd die!"

"I must get to France for safety. I can't danger Frank by sending him mail. And Dutch Billy leaves Holland no more; so he cannot bring letters. Remember Dutch Billy? He was Degroot-er in disguise, did you know?"

Cissy shook her head. "Be he a magnificent leader of men, as we thought? Does he cut a fine figure, and handsome?"

"No, a short dumpy fellow who thought to ruin a nation. His plan failed, and that's over. We must forget him, Cissy, and all we did for him."

"We simply *cannot* remain here in the dark!" Peg announced again in a distracted way. "A prey for any churl who comes along."

"Gil, say you will come to the Dissenters' meeting—now."

"No, flee with me—now!"

"I cannot marry an unbeliever."

"Be reasonable, both—" Peg began, then she tripped over the lantern. They were left in complete darkness.

"Link boy!" Gil cried. "Cissy, will you come? I dare not stay longer."

"No, no, I cannot. Wait awhile, my only love. I will wait too."

"I tell you the plague is upon London!"

A bright dot like a firefly came closer. A link boy swung his lantern.

"Cissy, marry me tonight! Now!"

Tears streamed down her face, and her whole body shook. "No, Gil, I promised the Lord. . . ."

He swore and dropped his arms. "You be not Cissy Nidd! I should be your only love. Are you bent on going to the Dissenters' meeting?"

Cissy's voice trembled. "I am."

He had to bend down to hear her. "Where? I'll escort you there."

"I can't reveal it. Gil, if you love me—go! Don't look back, please; I cannot betray them. Peg and I be there in two minutes or less! But don't look back. Gil, my love, God will bring us together again."

"I would do anything—almost—that you ask. This I can do. I won't look back, Cissy. And I'll find you again, I will."

He kissed her, turned, and strode away without looking back.

"Where will you go, my ladies?"

Cissy turned to the link boy, who grinned up at them. "Bear Inn on High Street," she replied. The beating of her heart almost suffocated her. "Six doors past is a chocolate house—I mean across the street—"

"The Bluebell," the boy prompted.

"Yes, yes, and upstairs—oh!" Cissy clapped her hand over her mouth.

"The Dissenters meet in the cheese loft," the boy said confidentially. "I see you know. My uncle attends there and I go with him."

"I can't imagine what you mean," Peg interrupted. "Just take us there."

"Yes, Mistress. To him that knocks, it shall be opened."

They followed him without speaking. The Bluebell wasn't far away, and once inside, Peg ordered chocolate and spice cakes. Cissy sat with her head leaning on one hand. She couldn't eat, and she hardly touched the hot drink. To see Gil again after so long; to see him and then have to bid him good-bye!

"I don't want to go to the meeting," she whispered, keeping her cloak tightly about her. "Let's go home; I am ill."

The owner crossed the small, cheerful room to greet them. There were no other guests in the place. "Ladies," he said softly, "I see you are much troubled."

"No, we are but tired," Peg replied.

Cissy rose. "Thank you, we will call a link boy and go now."

"*To him that knocks, it shall be opened.* Master Bunyan described both of you and told me to watch for you."

Cissy hesitated, then with a scraping motion she cleared the ringlets from her forehead and tied the scarf around her head to hide the rest of her hair. She used her glove to wipe the red paint from her cheeks. She and Peg waited while the owner locked the front door and blew out all but one candle. "Did anyone see you enter?" he asked.

"Not in this fog." Peg's voice shook, but she waited for Cissy to decide.

"We'd like to attend." Cissy pulled the hood of her cloak over her head. "*Narrow is the way, and few there be that enter.*"

They reached the cheese loft by climbing up a wooden ladder from inside a closet. The room was empty of imported merchandise. About thirty people sat on the floor, men together, women together. The only light came from a candle on a low table, and the windows had been pasted over with black paper.

The woman next to them reached out and clasped their hands. A woman next to Cissy kissed her on the cheek. Brother Doad was the Dissenting preacher. He knelt behind the low table, and in the candlelight Cissy saw a loaf of bread and a bowl of grape juice.

"On that same night in which the Lord was betrayed . . ." He recited the familiar words, and Cissy thought she had never heard them in a stranger setting. No brass altar rail, no plush cushion on which to kneel, no light on stained-glass windows.

The candle flame gleamed like a gold sovereign. Like true coin, thought Cissy. I want to be true coin, not false. It occurred to her that deciding for Christ was just the first step in a Christian life. There were other steps—oh, so many more. Saying no to the theater with its shameless audience. Saying no to Gil. She must witness to Peg and Trig.

Another thought occurred to her: she must forgive her father.

". . . my body which was broken for you," Brother Doad continued. "As I break this loaf." His hands tore the loaf in two, four, six, many pieces. ". . . So He is distributed to us, and we are to be broken in spirit before Him, willing to be broken for each other."

As Cissy watched, she didn't see bread; she saw a Man tormented and wracked, a Man who could have called for divine aid but would not. A Man who for love of her bore her punishment and gave up His breath.

A chunk of the loaf was handed her; she broke off a bit and passed it to the next woman.

". . . remember Me," she heard Brother Doad say, and she felt she would burst with love for Him. "Thou art my love," the man quoted, and Cissy knew she needed no other love.

The bowl was passed around. Each one drank from it. "One faith, one Lord, one Church but diversity among its members." The ancient words of the Anglican creed came to mind. And if she chose to sit on the floor in the dark in a cheese loft, was it any of the government's business?

The faces around her were in shadow, and she kept her hood pulled close to her eyes. We don't know each other, she thought. I could be sitting next to a servant girl, a Billingsgate fish woman, a physician's wife, or a highborn lady. Me, Cissy Nidd, the jailer's daughter. I belong.

She closed her eyes while the others were supping the cup. Oh, my Lord, do answer my questions and satisfy all my longings.

Brother Doad received back the empty bowl. "Instead of the Scripture I had chosen, I will read a verse from the book of James, the first chapter, the seventeenth verse. I feel there may be someone here tonight who needs assurance of the salvation they already possess."

Cissy's fingernails cut into her hands as she strained to hear every quiet word.

"God is the Father, with whom is no variableness, neither shadow of turning. This is in Holy Writ. God will not turn His back to look for our sins. Not even His shadow moves. He will never change. *Jesus Christ, the same yesterday, today, forever.*"

Cissy fixed her eyes on the candle flame, now thin and weak, which took its strength from the wick. A great light burst into her soul and drove out the chilling doubts. *God doesn't turn His back!*

Lord, Have Mercy on Us

Attendance at The Black Pot usually fell away in the winter months, but this winter was even worse, Peg declared.

Cissy was helping her clean out the pantry so they could keep the rat population down. "The Black Pot would not close, would it?" she asked. "Whatever would we do? I'd not go home to Bedford!"

Peg discovered the edges of the sugar loaves nibbled and rat droppings in the coffee beans. "Drat! What pesky creatures! Even the cats are afeared of them. We need a dog, Cissy. No, we wouldn't close; Trig has money laid by. It's war with Holland that scares people. They're afeared to spend a shilling. The plague, though, be stayed in Holland."

Cissy wiped the shelves with a wet rag. "Well, thank the Lord for that! Do you know I found a litter of baby rats in my woolen stockings?"

"Dearie, dearie me. I hope you threw them out. Cissy, the plague be finished in Holland, but it's moved to England. We hear but little—only what the government wants us to hear. The

Dutchmen who fight the English, *they* be recovered from all that sickness, but *we* be just beginning. England may have to sue for peace.''

Cissy found a crock of pickles without a lid, and yes, there was a dead rat floating in it. ''Mistress Parfrey next door told me she found a pair of rats honeymooning in her best wig!''

Peg's loud laughter boomed out. ''That's rare! I'll tell Trig of that! He was down on the riverside last week and near to have drowned of rats, there were so many. Be sure everything has a lid on it and hang the onions nigh to the roof.''

By Christmas, Cissy still had not heard a word from Gil. Were it not for my Lord, I'd give over and die, she often thought. I feel I have almost more than my share of grief.

She often saw Peg reading a Bible, sitting alone, but Peg said that she wanted to keep her religion to herself. ''I'd never forsake Divine Service,'' she told Cissy. ''But I like the music and the talk now, though I don't understand it all.''

''Maybe you like it better because you have Christ in your heart,'' Cissy said. ''The service hasn't changed; mayhap you have changed. Do you surely trust Jesus only for salvation?''

Peg thought for a minute. ''Yes, I do. But I don't want to worship in a cheese loft!''

Cissy laughed. ''As long as you understand that attending the service and taking part does not forgive sins, I suppose each may worship where he chooses. I be too upset with what the ruling church has done to England and its people.''

''Don't quarrel on it.'' Peg closed the Bible and went off to bake pies.

In February, England declared war upon the Dutch. Fewer customers than ever came to The Black Pot. Cissy had plenty of time to read her Bible and keep a diary. 'Twill be for Gil, she decided. When we are together and wed, he will know all I've learned during this dreary time.

Taking up her quill pen, she saw that a rat had gnawed the tip away. Someone hammered at the door. Too early for a diner. She sighed and got up to answer.

"Frank!"

"Cissy, dearest Cissy! How good to see you at last!" Her brother swung her around in a circle, hugging her tightly. "Cissy, I ran away. I knew you were here; Master Bunyan told me. I'll work hard and only ask for a corner to lie in at night and a heel of a loaf."

Cissy looked at her brother, now twenty-two, as handsome a man as any of the young lawyers who took the air around St. Paul's.

"You'll fare better than that. What of—of Pa and Harold?"

"Fled to Holland with the money."

"I don't want any; it's money got by crime," Cissy said quickly. Then she remembered her dowry money—what she still had left of it—buried under the lilac bush. She must give it back. Back to whom? Mayhap give it to the parson in Bedford or leave it at the mayor's house.

"What of Master Bunyan?"

"He lies in Bedford Jail with bad rheumatism, and the new jail keeper is Master Barnhouse, who is no friend to him. Had Master Bunyan money, he would buy his way out of jail. Last year he wrote the story of his conversion, *Grace Abounding to the Chief of Sinners*. I read parts of it, and I almost thought it was about me. Betsy and the children near starve in the winter. My heart goes out to them."

Cissy poured him a hot drink. "And what of Nellie?"

Frank turned his head away to study a fly crawling up the wall. "She is an Anglican, who never did a wrong thing in her life. And I, a Dissenter with a background of crime. Reconcile that if you can."

"What! You, Frank, a Dissenter. A real Christian born from above and following Jesus?"

"Aye. Master Bunyan led me to Him. I was never even a good Anglican, you know, just went to Divine Service to keep within the law." A rat ran across the kitchen floor, and he threw a knife at it.

"God will call Nellie to Himself as we pray for her."

"Now here's something will make you jump for very gladness." Frank pulled several folded sheets out of his pocket.

Cissy knew at once. "From Gil? Oh, Frank, where is he? How is he? We must pray for him to know Christ as we do. Give me the letter, do. Don't tease."

She laid her cheek on the pages of the letter and closed her eyes. A long letter, almost as good as having him near. She buried it in the pocket of her gown for later.

"Frank, we must talk a little. Tell me, have you heard of the plague anywhere in England? I be so afraid of it."

"Aye, in among the poor, where refugees and beggars live in shacks. And it's outside the city walls around the pools and marshes where drainage ditches run into the river. Just among the poor."

"I see. Frank, do you want to hear from my diary what has happened in the past six months? Not that it is earthshaking news, just things that took my fancy. On Christmas night a strange new moving star was seen in the heavens, a comet passing right over London. A faint-glowing star, slow, like a sick person—or sickness. You know how you feel when you've been abed and can't stand up, with a heavy head and dull eyes."

Frank cracked his cup down on his saucer. "And you be obsessed with the plague, I declare! I tell you, it's only among the poor."

"Oh, dear, you've chipped the saucer! I'll not mention it again. Will you have some more coffee?"

"I will, indeed. Butter me another slab of that good bread. I've been starving for your cooking, such as it was."

Cissy laughed and referred again to her diary. "I've had plenty of time to take up writing. Perchance the world will hear of me someday! I read the papers and borrow a book once in a while from Mistress Parfrey. Now then—a little trading post of the colonies in North America has been captured from the Dutch and renamed New York after the Duke.''

''Never heard of any New York and don't care. Have you no more exciting news?''

''The way to find news is to converse with the merchants at the Exchange, a place I've never seen, what with being only a female.''

Frank studied her and a smile curved his lips. ''Do you know, Cis, you talk like a man but you don't look like a man. I like the way your hair is pinned up high with a lace cap on top. You're right comely!''

''Thank you, I'm sure.'' Cissy felt for the letter in her pocket. ''Frank, you must know, then, that Gil and I are promised. Do you see him often?''

''No, he be in danger again. He used to come disguised as a pilgrim to speak with Master Bunyan when he was permitted to counsel such people. Now, Master Bunyan can see no one. I've always been fond of Gil Turpin. It's been a long time for you, Cis, loving and waiting. A long time for Gil too.''

''Yes, a long time. It's been forever.'' Cissy kept her head down, carefully filling in all the ovals of the letters in her diary with ink as a child would do. ''I must go back to Bedford someday soon. I keep putting it off, praying for courage.''

''Back to Bedford!''

''Yes, and to jail most likely. There is a good deal of money I kept out for my dowry, buried under the lilac bush. I want to return it to someone. I can't keep it.''

''You can't tell of the counterfeiting! What of me? Would you betray your brother?''

Cissy looked up sadly. ''No, that is on your conscience and for you to decide.''

''God has forgiven all that!''

"Aye, He has put our sins behind His back—and He doesn't turn around. 'Tis balm for a hurting conscience. But the Bible tells us to confess and make things right."

"I haven't a farthing! Pa and Harold took it all!"

"Then I must go alone. Think of Zacchaeus in the Bible, paying back four times what he defrauded."

"Think of me!" Frank shoved the cups aside and jumped up, striding angrily to the front door. "I'm going for a walk to get real news! Speak no more to me of going back to Bedford! Or of the plague!"

Peg returned from buying cabbage and turnips at the waterfront. "Why, I just saw your brother! Why is he in such a temper? He passed me on the Bridge without so much as a 'by your leave'!"

"You are not at fault, Peg dear; we had a disagreement. Frank is pleased to stay with us, if you don't object. Will you wash the greens if I take to my room for a spell? I have a letter from my young man."

"From the highway—" Peg caught herself. "God be praised, for I wish you happiness from the bottom of my heart!"

Cissy drew the curtains around her bed and unfolded the letter.

Darling, darling Cissy Nidd,

Her eyes began to fill with tears. He wasn't angry with her. He loved her. If he'd written naught else, she'd wait forever and be glad.

I have been in France.

He described the people, the food, the buildings and landscapes. He was well. The life of highwayman was over.

I am penniless, my little love. I have made good my bad deeds, and the fortune is gone. I have been studying architecture and should be able to settle in France with a good job, when you arrive.

When I arrive? Cissy read ahead swiftly. He was a Christian, born into God's family! Her Gil was a Dissenter. All thanks to Master Bunyan. Such news almost made her dizzy.

There was more in the letter, all about France and his purchase of a Bible and meeting Dissenters. He even knew of the secret meeting places in England.

Cissy read the letter twice more, then slipped it inside the pillow covering where her head would rest on it each night. Opening her Bible, she turned to the Psalms, where she had started chapter ninety-one. How glorious to think that at this very moment Gil might be opening a Bible too.

But what of returning to Bedford? Perhaps now it wasn't necessary? She read on, hoping for guidance. *". . . under the shadow of the Almighty . . . my refuge and my fortress."* And verse three, *"Surely he shall deliver thee from . . . the noisome pestilence."* Parts of verses stood out for her on the page: *"Thou shalt not be afraid for the terror by night . . . nor for the pestilence that walketh in darkness."* Her eyes skipped down to the tenth verse.

There it was! The plague! *"Neither shall any plague come nigh thy dwelling."* Was that a promise to all Christians everywhere? Surely not, for she knew plagues of the past had stricken Christian and pagan alike.

She must go to the Dissenters' meeting and ask. She prayed for her headstrong brother in his newfound faith. For Peg, who was now a real Christian. For Trig, who wanted naught to do with religion. For dearest Gil, of course. For Harold. For Pa, that someday she could find it in her heart to forgive him, for the bitterness was a thorn in her soul.

Frank returned several hours later, his anger over Bedford forgotten. "I saw a solemn sight," he said to the two women in the kitchen. "And I beg your pardon, Cissy, for I was wrong. I walked all over, and in Drury Lane I first saw it. A house with a foot-high cross painted on the door, and over it the words, 'Lord, have mercy on us!' "

"The plague!" Cissy stopped stirring the gravy and looked at Peg.

"Every so often somebody dies of plague," Peg said. "What of it?"

"Not this time," Frank said solemnly. "Forty-eight dead last week of plague and one hundred twelve this week. The passing bell tolled even as I went by. And the cross on the door was on a rich dwelling."

"I tell you the plague be confined to the slums," Peg snapped. "Put a piece of garlic in your mouth for protection when you go out."

"Frank, pray don't go near those places!" Cissy thickened the gravy with flour and added drippings from the pan. "Only this morning I read in Psalm 91 of the plague. Lord, deliver us!"

"Don't fuss so over naught." Peg sliced up the roast beef and put it on a shelf by the fire to keep warm. "You two get along to your meeting, now, and be careful! Trig is out buying coals. Take the shopping baskets and buy some cabbages, so people don't suspect you are going to a Dissenters' meeting in broad daylight."

"Won't you come, Peg?"

"Not me. One time was enough. I think it wrong to hide in the dark and sit on the floor, everybody interpreting the Bible as he pleases. Denying the church and the sacraments and the clergy that God puts over us."

Out on London Bridge, Cissy and Frank both carried baskets on their arms. Cissy told her good news. "You come to France with us. Gil would make you welcome. Someday we'll come back when all is forgotten of his deeds."

"I'll think on it, should the plague worsen."

When Frank bought a pound of walnuts, Cissy bought cabbages. She'd knotted a crushed clove of garlic in her handkerchief and tucked it into the neck of her dress.

"Whewwww!" Frank mocked her, holding his nose. "The authorities only need follow the scent to find the beautiful law-breaker! Follow the scent to find the Dissenters!"

He laughed so hard he tripped and slid into the ditch in the middle of the street. "Now look at my shoes!"

"Frank, do be serious and don't say 'Dissenter' so loud. Where is this meeting you've found?"

"Master Bunyan told me. It's safer than going over into Southwark. Just follow me and don't itch to run ahead. We must dawdle along, shop, then quick as a jump-jack pop into a certain doorway."

"Not in the plague neighborhood, I trust."

"Indeed not. Ho, didn't I see a pile of cabbages at The Black Pot, a mound like a pyramid of cannonballs?"

Cissy patted the three green heads in her basket. "You did. We don't need more, but what shall I buy if not cabbage?"

"Buy light goods to carry, as I did. Buy some stationery for your diary book for your true love."

"Oh, brave!" Cissy laughed and took his arm. There was a love-link between them now, she thought, this brother who was so much like herself. Harold she never did understand. He'd scarcely bothered to notice her all her life.

Cissy felt light as the dust from butterfly wings. The sky was laced with wispy clouds, and the plague seemed as far away as Bedford. Within the hour they would be with other believers, and in daylight she would see and know who they were.

She yearned for Christian friends, to recognize Christians on the street. She could stop for an innocent chat, perhaps be invited to their homes for dinner. She longed to recognize goodwives, to smile at them and with her eyes say, "God bless you, dear; we know whom we have believed, and He is able."

Partway up Fish Hill, they saw a man in a velvet jacket and trailing black cloak, carrying a red wooden chest. A long line of poor people held out their pennies to him. As they came closer,

Cissy heard him chant: "Tablets to prevent plague! Charms and amulets! Signs of the zodiac! Two for tuppence!"

A woman in a topsy-turvy bonnet cried out, "Good Master Magician, will the plague come here? Tell us truly!"

"Of a certainty it will," he assured her, snapping together his shiny false teeth. "The plague is already here and fast spreading. Best to be prepared, good folk."

All the housewives and workmen pushed and shoved to get closer to the wise man. Money was thrust at him so freely that his two hands could scarce handle all the profit.

"Gulled of their money, poor souls," said Frank.

"Have they no comfort for their fears?" Cissy asked, watching them swarm around the man in black. "Do such people at least attend Divine Service to know there is a God?"

"Don't worry your head over them," said Frank. "They be such low class."

At the top of the hill, Frank turned left. "Look yonder, Cis. Do you see the row of small houses and a sign, 'Brick Court'? 'Tis a small garden where folks lucky to know about it can wander in and pick flowers or sit by a fountain. Pass straight through it and out the other side, which puts us onto Cornmeal Lane. After that, follow me sharp and do as I do. We'll be going through a bake shop."

They passed a lace school and the children on their noon free time playing at "one-two-buckle-my-shoe" or sitting on the grass eating bread and cheese.

Brick Court was tucked between two cottages. They walked through, admiring the flowers. Just before they stepped onto Cornmeal Lane, Frank looked all around, then hurried into a bakery.

Two women were picking up their finished loaves. When the door shut behind them, Frank addressed the baker. "Master Johnson, we do not bring loaves nor pick them up."

"No?" He gave them a sharp look. He was not much older than Frank, with light hair and a broad, serious face.

"No, we seek living bread, the Bread that came down from heaven."

Master Johnson left his work at the fireplace ovens and looked up and down the lane. "Go through yonder door down to the coal hole."

Down the steps and into a cellar, Cissy climbed, past chests of grain. Due to the six-month drought, Master Johnson had stored barrels of drinking water in long rows. Behind them was the wooden door to the coal hole, with a foot of coal piled against it.

Frank pulled at the door's brass ring, and the coal slid aside. He and Cissy squeezed through the narrow opening. The coal was banked around the sides of the room. A dozen people sat on a long bench.

"Frank Nidd, living at The Black Pot on the Bridge, and my sister, Cissy," Frank introduced them. The other folk murmured their names. Cissy recognized a tailor from the Bridge. Next to him were two women who shopped at a fish stall where she often went for the best mussels.

Master Collins was the Dissenting minister. He led the people in praying for rain. Except for a light shower in April, no rain had fallen for six months.

Then he read and explained a portion of Holy Scripture, the fourth chapter of Philippians, dwelling upon verses 6 and 7: *Be careful for nothing; but in every thing by prayer and supplication with thanksgiving let your requests be made known unto God. And the peace of God, which passeth all understanding, shall keep your hearts and minds through Christ Jesus.*

He asked if there were any questions. "Will the plague come to us?" a woman wanted to know. "How shall we endure?"

"Will God use the plague to judge England?" asked a man.

"And if our neighbor fall with the plague, are we to succor him and bring death upon ourselves?"

Cissy looked around, surprised. Ordinary people, asking questions of a minister, questioning the meaning of Scripture! Suddenly she felt almost inspired. She would do it! She, too, had a right to speak! "Sir, how can we be kept from even thinking of a horror such as the plague? We are but frail, sinful humans. I know my own thoughts return to the plague over and over; I fear it that much."

She could sense Frank's alarm because she had spoken aloud in public, but Master Collins was not taken aback. "I will read on to verse eight," he said. "The solution lies not in ridding our minds of unwholesome thoughts only to have an empty mind. Verse eight tells us to fill our minds so full of good thoughts there will be no room for plague thoughts.

"In place of false rumors, think upon truth. In the stead of deception, think of things honest. Pure thoughts instead of impurity. Lovely, instead of the unlovely. Think on the good reports instead of the frightening reports."

Master Johnson had descended into the coal hole and stood behind them. When the meeting was over, he whispered to Frank, who then turned to her. "Cissy, allow me to introduce Clarence Johnson, the baker we met upstairs. He owns this bakery. Clarence, this is my sister, Cissy. Cis, Clarence knows Master Bunyan."

Cissy looked into a pair of blue eyes and a pleasant face.

"How do ye do?" he said, grasping her hand instead of making a formal bow.

Cissy blushed and found she wasn't able to pull her hand away. It must be the Dissenter way of greeting. "Pleased to m-meet you, I'm sure," she stammered.

"Dear sister, you be welcome here anytime," he said.

The other Dissenters left, two and three at a time, with five minutes between departures. Master Johnson sauntered through Brick Court as though taking the air, but he was watchful. He signaled to the Dissenters for their discreet leave-taking.

Before he bade farewell to Cissy and Frank, he said, "I fear the government knows more than they tell us about the plague. The great fair near Cambridge has been canceled. Likewise, the

St. James Fair at Bristol. The lawyers of Middle Temple court have all fled to the country.''

"I mind me of the most awful stories," Cissy volunteered. "In the fourteenth century, one-third of Bedford died in the plague. The doors stood ajar; the meals still hot on the tables. The families lay dead where they had fallen."

"Softly, softly," Master Johnson said, noting her disquiet. "Think of what our pastor told us. God is in the storm, the earthquake, war and famine, along with His people. He is present with us in the plague if it comes."

They parted, and Frank said hotly, "I do beg you don't mention plague again, Cis. You're depressing as mourner's weeds. Who knows, speaking of it may draw it closer. By the by, did you note how anxious Johnson was to make your acquaintance? That bake shop is his own, you know."

Cissy flashed him an angry look. She would never even look at another one except Gil. They reached a corner where they could see down four streets. They heard a commotion in the direction of the Royal Exchange and stopped to stare. People were scattering in all directions, as though pirates had been sighted.

A mighty exodus of men on horseback surged toward them. Cissy saw wagons crammed with household goods and people on foot. Dozens of vehicles throttled the narrow streets.

Rich merchants leaned out of their coach windows, roaring, "Get on with you! Get to the city gates and away!"

Though it was daytime, Cissy noticed that many of the houses had their shutters tightly closed.

"What is it? What's happening?" she asked Frank.

The outcry and clamor of the hordes of people struggling in the streets formed itself into a single cry: "The plague! The plague!"

Bring Out Your Dead

Cissy woke out of a sound sleep, thinking that a thunderstorm was trouncing London. Blasts of thunder rolled across the Thames and echoed down London Bridge. Thank God for the rain, she thought sleepily. Now the streets will be washed clean. The cooler air might perk Peg up and make her feel better.

The noise moved closer, hammering The Black Pot. "Why, it's not thunder!" She sat up in bed and groped for her clothes. Someone was knocking at the front of the inn. Bam! Bam! Hammer thuds against the door.

Peg stayed in bed. She'd been feeling weak lately. Trig and Frank ran downstairs, their night slippers flapping on the steps.

"Ho! Soho! Stop there! Help, constable! Madmen! Frank, call out the window for help! Burglars!" Trig shouted.

A thumping and drubbing began at the back door. Cissy, half-dressed, tied a big wrapper around her and ran to Peg's bedroom window. She could see the middle of the street, but the upper story hung out over the lower story, as all the houses were built. She couldn't see what was happening.

She ran downstairs and bumped into Frank running up. "Scream out the window!" he said. "Two men are padlocking the doors so we can't get out!"

Cissy threw up the little window by the front door. "Good neighbors, please stop! Stop! What is the meaning of this?"

The workman finished hammering and went around to the back door to help his friend. The man out front carried a gun and touched his cap politely to Cissy. "Morning, Mistress, we're indeed sorry to do this so early in the morning, but Dr. Ganer reported Mistress Metcalf has the plague upon her. All infected houses must be shut up for forty days."

Cissy leaned out until she lay flat upon the window box. "No! Peg does not have the plague! She is ill from the great heat this summer and she took a fever! The doctor was here! Ask him!"

"No need to ask. Dr. Ganer went straight to the parish officer and told his findings. He didn't want to alarm the rest of the family—but you must know it now. Your mistress has the plague."

Trig threw open the upstairs window. "You can't lock us up for forty days to die in here! 'Tis the same as murder!"

"'Tis the law," retorted the man. "I'm the day watchman, and I will stand guard from six o'clock of the morning 'til ten tonight. The other man will stand the night watch. We're to fetch you food and run your errands, but you may not come out and spread infection. There be a nine o'clock curfew and all public places are closed. Seven hundred persons died last week. The king and his court are fled to Oxford. Lord, have mercy upon us!"

He pronounced the words even as he painted them on the door above a red cross.

Cissy ran up to Peg's room. "Peg! Get up, do, and show yourself to these knaves! Peg, aren't you dressed yet?"

Peg lay on her back breathing heavily. Her face and arms were red with fever, and she held one hand to her neck. "There's a boil or a lump," she said. "Ah, how it hurts! Pains terrible.

Call the doctor again. I been sick in the night. My head's tight as a drum and there's a drummer a-beating on it.''

Cissy examined the boil. It was red and hard, the size of a penny. "I'll put a poultice on it right away. Peg, dear, can't you get up so the men can see you're not too sick?"

Peg only closed her eyes and moaned. Trig ran into the room. "Come, get up, Peg! Come, my good woman! Alas, we be locked into our own home! Peg, get up, that's a love!''

"She is sick, but it is only a boil. Ask the watchman what to do. Will the doctor come again?''

"Not if it's plague," Frank said in her ear. "Cissy, we'll break out of here tonight and go home to Bedford.''

Cissy wrung her hands, watching Peg anxiously. "Nobody is allowed outside the city gates without a Certificate of Health, I heard. And I couldn't leave Peg here sick.''

She threw open the lattice and called down. "Watchman! What do doctors recommend to open a boil?''

"No boil; she's got a plague token. Too late for her. I'll read you the paper we was given to carry in our pockets: 'From the Royal College of Surgeons. Put a fig steeped in treacle into a hollow onion. Wrap in wet paper and roast near embers. Apply it hot on top of the tumor.' And pray God the plague token doesn't turn black,'' he added.

"I'll make the poultice.'' Trig ran to the cellar to fetch onions. "Shut all the windows,'' he called over his shoulder. "I heard a neighbor say plague travels through the air. Stop up all the cracks and burn some old boots in the fireplace. Cissy, make a twist of paper to stop up the keyhole.''

Cissy ran to obey. What would Master Bunyan do? she thought. Lord, have mercy! Only last week Peg felt so good she carried soup to poor Mistress Trumbull three doors down. Oh! Oh! They say Mistress Trumbull had the plague and now she's in her grave! The plague must have gone right from her pores into Peg's pores.

When the onion poultice was hot, she tied it onto Peg's boil. Peg groaned in pain. She couldn't take even a sip of water without becoming sick. All day long she lay in bed.

Cissy ran up and down the steps, heating onion after onion, hoping to bring the boil to a head. She lost count of the hours, knowing only that the street was strangely quiet; occasionally a cart rattled by, but hardly any people walked about.

She bathed Peg and changed her nightclothes, then sprinkled vinegar around the room to purify the air. Sitting in a chair by Peg, she fell asleep from exhaustion. She must have slept for hours when she felt Frank shake her arm.

"Trig is gone, saved himself. When the watch changed at ten and both men talked a few minutes out front, he let himself down from the back window on a rope and took to the river. Only the Lord knows where he'll go. Maybe he'll pay to live on one of the little boats. He cleaned all the money out of the drawer."

"Trig gone?" Cissy rubbed her eyes and sat up straight. "Oh, Frank, how will we manage here? If Peg—if Peg—oh, I can't say it, but if we're left alone, boarded up for forty days, and one of us takes sick! Lord, have mercy! I can't make my brains work! I'm fair out of my wits. What would Master Bunyan do?"

"Master Bunyan be safer than we are," Frank said grimly. "And I think you should be asking the Lord for help. Look to Peg well and see that you get the boil to break."

Frank frowned thoughtfully. "We have plenty of flour for baking, but no meat or fresh food. The watchman is paid by the parish to fetch us whatever we need if I can find some money. He says many of the Anglican ministers fled to the country, and the Dissenting pastors are preaching openly in their churches. Thousands jam in, standing in the aisles, hanging in at the windows, such is their hunger for the Word of God. The poor are finally hearing the way of salvation."

"Frank, what of Peg? She goes by the Prayer Book and Divine Service; yet she told me of her complete faith in Jesus as her Savior. Shall I speak to her while she is suffering so?" Cissy asked.

"Nay, let her sleep." He paced the floor, back and forth, to and fro. "Already I feel like I'm in jail. Can we get a Dissenting pastor to visit her?"

"We dare not ask that of the watchman. We can only pray that help comes to us."

Cissy went to sit by Peg's side again. When she bathed her, she noted a small black mark like a mole in Peg's armpit. And three more marks were on her inner leg.

"Lord, have mercy!" Cissy prayed. "It is the plague."

Day by day Peg grew worse. Across the street from The Black Pot, Master Jones, a furniture maker, fired off a gun blast every hour to clear the air. The funeral bell of the church at the foot of London Bridge tolled all day long.

"Eighteen hundred died this week," said the watchman. "A solemn fast was declared by the Lord Mayor of London, asking people to repent of their sin and pray God to end the plague."

Peg died three days later. Her face and neck had been paralyzed for days and her sight gone.

Cissy and Frank wrapped her in the bed covers, and when the Dead Cart came by, they carried her out. "Bring out your dead!" the driver cried under each window.

The watchman unlocked the door long enough for the Burying Man to drag the body outside. "No funeral, no following to the grave," he said. "All that be forbidden now."

Cissy wept and watched the horse-drawn cart stop at other doors on the Bridge. "Bring out your dead!" People died at so fast a rate that the Burying Man was heard at all hours.

Cissy asked the watchman to buy her some herbs from a shop, and he replied, "I wouldn't touch your money. Hand me a crock of vinegar out the window and I'll set it by the door. Drop your money down into it. I'll fish it out after the plague has time to be melted off."

"My brother and I be well. Cannot we step out for air?"

"Forty days," the man replied.

Cissy cooked meals, spent hours with her Bible, and sewed. Frank fretted and fumed and tried to think up ways to outfox the watchman. They both sat for long hours in the upper windows, looking down on the street or river. Were I ever left alone in this place, I'd go mad, Cissy thought.

As August dragged on, the heat worsened and corpses piled up in the street. One week, six thousand died. The plague struck so swiftly that people died where they fell. Grass and weeds sprang up between the cracks of roads that once were well traveled.

Cissy gazed at the river. No foreign ships were in, nothing stirring but small boats going back and forth. The commerce of a nation had come to a dead stop.

Frank gave the watchman some silver spoons to sell, and he bought a supply of sulphur which they threw into the fireplace to purify the air. An hour later, Frank was lying on a lounge, lying on one side with his eyes closed, when he said, "Oh, the air smells so sweet, Cis, like the gilly flowers and roses back home in your garden."

With a cry Cissy ran to kneel by him, her hand on his forehead. That was the first warning sign of plague—the afflicted imagined that he smelled sweetness. "Frank, are you feeling well? You didn't take a mouthful of food today, and yesterday you only drank water."

"I'm so tired of being shut up. Makes my head ache. How much longer to go?"

"Not long, Frank. Is that a bruise by your chin?"

"Aye, it's sore, but it's nothing. The vile smell of the sulphur kills my appetite. Yet, there is a sweetness in the air. . . ."

"Loosen your shirt and let me see your arms. Please, Frank."

He was so weak she had to help him remove his shirt. In the armpit were two dusky swellings, each the size of a shilling. She was silent with terror, not wanting him to know.

"Just let me sleep," he said. "Throw a cover over me, for there's a draft coming down the chimney."

That night Cissy woke to find him stalking the room in an icy chill, delirious with pain.

"Lord, have mercy on us!" Cissy paced the floor with him, pleading with him to lie down. "Oh, God, what shall I do? Frank, let me put a poultice on the boils. Please take to your bed and I'll call the doctor."

He knocked her aside and she fell to the floor, skinning her elbows. Frank threw himself down on the lounge and buried his face in the pillow. "I can't stand the pain! Get me Trig's pistol!"

"No! No!" She ran upstairs, found the gun, and threw it down to the startled watchman. "Call a doctor, for my brother is very sick! For the love of God, help us!"

"Doctors all dead or gone," said the watchman. "Only one apothecary left, and he's away over beyond Westminster. Ten thousand homes shut up in London. Give your brother strong drink for the pain."

"I have nothing—nothing! No money, no medicine! I gave you all the cutlery long ago. Have mercy, as you are a Christian! My brother will die piecemeal unless you help. Can you run and ask Master Clarence Johnson, a baker on Cornmeal Lane, to come? He lives at the corner of the Lane and Brick Court."

"No money, eh? What's that jewelry a-hanging out of your collar?"

Cissy covered the ruby with her hand. "There's three lace tablecloths left—"

"I'll take the ruby."

"There's a framed scene painted by a master—"

"Throw down the ruby!"

"Oh, have mercy, sir! Take the wheat that's left!"

"Won't take food out of a plague house. Drop down the ruby."

"Do you promise, as God is listening, to call Master Johnson?"

"I promise."

The ruby fell on the grass like a drop of blood. The watchman snatched it up and polished it on his breeches. "It's a real one, ain't it? All right, I'm off to fetch the baker."

Cissy rested her head on the window. Gil, it doesn't matter. I don't need a ruby to keep me true. Gil, are you safe from the plague? I pray God to keep you.

Master Johnson was there within the hour carrying a package of tablets and a bottle of plague water. "Drink the water to prevent the illness," he said, looking up at her in great worry. "Make a paste of the tablets and spread it on the boils." He handed up the package tied to the end of a rod. "And remember, Cecelia, I will be praying for you both."

"Oh, thank you, thank you. May it do something to help poor Frank." She received the package with shaking hands.

"Cissy, the watchman in his haste dropped a necklace in my yard. Know you ought of it? I suspect some poor soul paid him with her last valuable."

"Oh, it's mine! It's mine, on my word! Keep it safe for me 'til this trial be over! Then my love and I will have something left to begin life with."

She ignored his sorrowful look, closed the window, and went to see Frank again. The plague boils on his neck were hard and black. Cissy followed the baker's instructions, but Frank threw off the bandage with the poultice and struck at her with his fists. When at last he fell into a deep swoon, Cissy dragged the trundle bed downstairs by his bed and collapsed upon it.

Night after night she tended him, day after day, snatching sleep whenever he slept. "Oh, merciful and loving God, don't leave me alone here! I couldn't bear being locked up alone!"

How long could a body go without food, without a drop of water, as Frank did? When she looked at him that night, his face was bloated and his lips blue. He didn't recognize her.

"Lord, have mercy!" Cissy prayed aloud. "I don't know what else to do!"

She dozed, half-awake, half-napping, on the trundle bed, thinking of how she missed Master Bunyan and his advice. I'm being tested by God, she mused. Master Bunyan is not here, and I must never look to him again in place of the Lord.

"Lord Jesus, I want to draw near and worship You! Oh, I want to know You better and speak to You from my heart and walk by faith when I cannot understand."

No other idols. The Bible words drifted into her sleepy thoughts. Have I made an idol of Master Bunyan?

She made herself remember all the colored pictures of Jesus in the books. But they weren't Jesus; nothing could picture Him. "Lord, I'll look to You alone," she prayed. "I'll come direct to You in all things, especially in this awful time."

"You will need Me in the days to come," He seemed to say in her soul. Another verse from Scripture rose in her mind: *In all their affliction, he was afflicted. . . .* She imagined His face: thin, red with fever, covered with plague boils. . . .

Suddenly Cissy sat up, startled by the rustling of bats in the chimney. The night was far advanced. She lit a candle and leaned over her brother's bed. Frank was dead.

The Great Fire

The plague months turned London topsy-turvy. Thousands died or fled the city. The Black Pot was boarded up as a plague house until men from the health office could burn sulphur in the rooms to fumigate them. Cissy was left without a roof for her head, without food or money.

Cissy heard it cried in the street that the earl of Craven needed a housekeeper. She went at once to his mansion on the edge of the city where the plague had not been so bad.

The earl lived at the bottom of Drury Lane and had remained in London all through the plague, doling out money and food. Now he was helping business places to get a new start.

"Dear Lord Jesus," prayed Cissy as she lifted the heavy brass door knocker. "Do provide for me now, as You took care of Betsy Bunyan and the children all these years."

A servant answered and showed her into the earl's library, where a portly man with greying hair sat behind an oak desk.

Oh, the books! thought Cissy, trying not to stare all around her. I'd work for him just for the privilege of using the books!

She curtsied and told him of her work at The Black Pot. "In truth, sir, I do want to return when I am able. Perhaps by then I will have a friend come and help me.'' Gil, she thought. What a wonder should they together reopen the place where she had spent such happy days!

The earl nodded. ''I thank you for your honesty. I, myself, dined there marvelously many times on my way to Southwark. Mistress Nidd, I do believe that with your experience, you are the answer to my problems in the kitchen here. All my servants fled to relatives outside London and none came back.''

He named a sum that made her fill up with joy. ''Oh, I'd do it just to be able to open the books!'' she burst out.

He had noticed her interest. ''You may, at any time. I think I would like to finance the opening of The Black Pot—when your friend comes along. And, Mistress Nidd, do read the best Book of all when you've time.''

She followed his pointing finger to a gilt-edged Bible on his desk. ''Oh! Oh, my! Are you a Di—'' No, she must not ask that question of anyone. ''Sir, have you news of—of the clergy and how they fare?''

He nodded thoughtfully. ''Most of the Anglican ministers fled to the country during the plague. The Dissenting pastors took over the pulpits and preached openly. The king ordered the Bishop of London to put a stop to this.

''The Five Mile Act was passed. No Dissenting preacher may live within five miles of any town or city. Thousands of pastors have fled London or are in hiding. And, of course, this applies to all England.''

Then Master Bunyan must hide or leave Bedford, Cissy thought. Ah, what terrible woes be upon this country. What work can the pastors get, living away from towns and cities?

In the earl's kitchen, she was mistress of six other servants newly hired. She taught them Peg's secret recipes—how to bake crustier loaves and the best way to serve up a broiled fish.

In a few months she had saved a nice amount of money. The day The Black Pot was put up for public auction, Cissy was there, the earl with her. With his kind aid, the place was put into her name.

That night she prayed, "Lord, now it needs only my dearest Gil. Surely he will come here looking for me. Bring him soon, please Lord."

The next Saturday was the busiest day of Cissy's whole week. Tom, the link boy, came back, and Cissy asked him to stay. Tom dug up a patch of grass out behind The Black Pot and planted turnips and parsnips to store through the winter.

In the afternoon, Nellie Farrel walked in, arriving from Bedford without warning. She was still dainty, and the merry, teasing eyes Cissy remembered were now resolute. Her indulgent father had given her a dowry of fifty pounds, but she still refused to stay at home.

"Cissy dear, I still grieve over Frank." They sat at the kitchen table while Tom waited on a few customers in the dining room. "Mistress Bret came back from a trip to London and told me you were here. I couldn't think of another place I'd wish to be except where Frank had lived. Cissy, will you have me?"

"You'll make a fine cook."

Within a month, Cissy was showing a profit in her ledger. She and Nellie went over the book regularly, entering expenses and income in two adjoining columns.

"Just fancy," said Nellie, "two women alone running a business."

"Two women plus Master Clarence Johnson," Cissy replied, making neat little entries in the ledger. "His bread and prayers keep our venture going. He has eyes for you, dear, and may it happen soon, though your dowry be spent on eggs and flour. I will repay you someday."

Nellie blushed and fussed with her blue checkered apron, wanting it just right in case anyone dropped by. "Master Johnson dines here for the good food, I'm sure."

"There be thirty other eating places between here and Cornmeal Lane."

"Nay, he comes to encourage our souls, since Pastor Collins was banished."

Cissy laughed and nodded wisely. "No, 'tis you who are the attraction. All the rich have returned to London now; so we be well off and you must set a wedding day."

"I must be asked first," said Nellie, looking pleased.

Cissy stopped to look out of the window at the river. Harbor traffic was almost back to normal. Ship carpenters and painters were hard at work again.

Outside in the street she could hear peddlers crying, "Ribbons and buttons!" and "Looking glasses with pearl handles!" London was a thriving seaport again.

"God have mercy on this nation!" Cissy suddenly drew a deep sigh and faced Nellie. "In spite of the plague, all the old places of sin are open again. The persecution of innocent Dissenters goes on. Did the government learn nothing from the plague? The king is laughed at, and his reign is called 'the frivolous court.' "

"I marvel at you, Cissy. You've turned scholar, what with sometimes quoting facts right out of your head. And the ideas you get from reading books!"

"I can thank the earl of Craven and his library. Someday you must see the books at Paternoster Row next to St. Paul's. When I have a little money to spare, we'll go there and see if we can buy a book or two."

"Does Master Bunyan sell his books there?"

"Sometimes. Do you know, I believe God is using him in prison more than if he were to preach. His books are loaned around where thousands may read them."

Nellie concentrated on the ledger. "We have plenty of supplies now. Shall we have fish or meat at noon?"

"Offer both," Cissy replied absently. "I'll leave you in charge today. Oh, and Master Johnson asked to dine with you this noon. I have set a table for two in the corner; now I shall take the air. Mayhap I will walk up to Pudding Lane and visit with Hannah Farnor.''

Nellie blushed rosy red. '' 'Tis too soon to think on Master Johnson.''

"Nonsense. You know I must go back to Bedford. I've told you my thoughts on it, and go I must. I must leave a letter for Pa with the new jailer should Pa come back or the jailer knows an address.''

"He wasn't kind to you,'' Nellie said slowly. "We all knew.''

"I must put my thoughts on paper for him. I have prayed God that I can forgive him all the old life, for he lost his wife young. She died a'saving me in the river, Nellie.''

"I know, dear. Is it safe for you to go back?''

"I trust in God. And there's an errand I must do.'' She thought of the money under the lilac bush. "My mind would be at ease were you and Master Johnson wed.''

Nellie hid her embarrassment in the ledger while Cissy took down her market basket and bonnet.

Walking down London Bridge, Cissy kept close to the house fronts as carts rattled past over the wooden planks. Six-story Tudor homes leaned wearily against each other. Masons and plumbers hurried by, carrying the tools of their trade.

Cissy shopped carefully, choosing fruit that would keep a week or so in the cold cellar. She walked slowly, to give Nellie time to think about Master Johnson. In days past, she had thought often about the ruby Gil had given her, but she thought also that perhaps Master Johnson had been forced to sell it to stay alive. Should she mention it today? She decided not to.

When she returned to The Black Pot, Master Johnson was taking his leave. "Cissy, do you remember the ruby on the necklace?'' he asked.

Her eyes widened. "Of course I remember. But if you had need to sell it. . . .''

"No, I didn't sell it. Pray listen.'' He lowered his voice. "Your true love has it and said that he himself will return it.''

Cissy picked her words carefully. This may be a trick to reveal she knew a highwayman. He didn't—couldn't—know Gil.

"And who is my true love, pray tell?"

"I told your story at the Dissenter meeting during the plague, and I asked prayer for you. A man was there. He was desperate enough to come into the plague area from the countryside, seeking *his* true love. This man was no longer a highwayman."

Gil! Gil Turpin! Cissy's heart near burst. "Oh, kindest Master Johnson, do not deceive me. Tell me true, for love of God."

"He's in London, Cissy, and within days you will see him. He has received a complete pardon from the king. It was partly due to the intercession of Master Pepys, whose life you once saved outside the theater. And it was partly due to Master Turpin's antics in the past, which amused the king. I am so happy for you, my dear sister." His pleasant face creased in a wide smile.

Cissy bid him good-bye and then hurriedly explained the whole story to Nellie in whispered snatches since guests were already seated next to the fire. Tom was stirring up the coals, for September was chilly. There were no more than ten guests; Cissy had closed off half the dining room so the two of them and young Tom could do all the work without hiring help.

After the last couple left, Cissy hung the "Closed" sign in the window. "I can think of naught else but Gil. May God be praised! Nellie, Tom, let's just sit by the fire and have Bible reading."

"May God forbid any more tragedy," Nellie said, curled up in a chair with a shawl over her feet.

Cissy gazed into the peaceful, smoldering coals in the fireplace. "We will stand firm in our faith and look to the Lord Jesus to keep us in peace. I do not expect any more disasters."

The day passed quietly as they read and dozed. In early evening Cissy closed all the shutters and made sure the two doors were barred before they slept. She and Nellie used the small upstairs bedroom, the other being shut up to save on coals. Tom slept by the kitchen fire.

After prayer with Nellie, Cissy dozed off to the creaking of The Black Pot sign swinging outside. An east wind must be blowing over the river, she thought drowsily. In a few days I will see Gil, and this time he will stay.

It seemed that no sooner had she shut her eyes than she heard Nellie cry, "Fire!" Jumping up at once, she called for Tom, but Nellie said, "Not here—at the foot of the Bridge!"

"The Bridge is afire! London Bridge is on fire!" The neighbors' screams stirred them to action. Cissy sent Tom out of the upstairs window and up onto the rooftop to look.

"It's coming this way fast!" he shouted. "Best run to Southwark!"

"Catch up my Bible and my books." Cissy tried to stay calm. "Tom, put our forks and spoons in a pillow wrapper—and anything else of value. Nellie, take the ledger and the money box!"

Tom climbed back into the room. "The barrels of tar and the timber on the waterfront are burning! The smoke is bad, but I think the fire came down Fish Hill. I saw a fire carriage with its pump, but it tipped and rolled end over end, down the hill—splash—into the river."

By now they could smell smoke and hear the frightened screams of people running past. "Listen!" Cissy stopped with one foot lifted on the steps. "The water wheel has stopped!"

"Burned!" cried Tom. "It's wooden, you know!"

Nellie appeared in the doorway dragging a sheet full of their possessions.

"That means no water to fight the fire—no water for anyone!"

Cissy looked out of the door and saw the Bridge engulfed in flame. Roofs and timbers and entire buildings cracked and fell, while some houses toppled off backward into the river.

"Run to Southwark!" she cried. "Leave everything behind! The fire is too close!"

Like the Judgment Day, the fire storm swept one-third of the way across the Bridge, a greedy downpour of liquid fire. Neighbors threw furniture and clothing down into the streets, and Cissy fell over the great piles. As the houses crackled, ash was spewed up into the air by the strong east wind and fell on everyone, singeing their clothes.

"Turn back! Southwark is afire!" The crowd turned and crushed the people running behind them.

"Oh, God, which way? Which way?" Cissy clung to Nellie and Tom as they huddled in the doorway of The Black Pot.

"Jump into the river!" shouted some men.

"Even heaven is on fire!" a woman screamed.

A man grabbed Cissy's arm. "Don't stay here, Mistress! Sparks blew across to Southwark and set a stable afire. Fire is coming both ways. Can you swim?"

"No," she gasped. "What shall we do?"

But he was gone, lost in the river of people that ran in both directions.

"Look, look!" Tom pointed down the street. The flames had stopped by a vacant area close by The Black Pot. After consuming everything that would ignite, the fire was burning itself out. Then the wind veered from east to southwest, and they saw the fire spread into the heart of London.

Cissy sank down on the doorstep and only then did she realize that her shoes were smoking hot and the soles of her feet burned.

Homeless people pushed into the inn until Cissy was forced to bar the door against any more. "The fire in Southwark is out," Tom reported. "The men say it's safe to go there for refuge."

Some of the people left The Black Pot to seek relatives across the Bridge, but Cissy and Nellie fed the rest, twenty-five in all. Soldiers were sent in from other counties to keep order and distribute food. Still, the fire burned across London. That night Cissy climbed out on the rooftop to see if the fire would spare St. Paul's and the booksellers around it.

London was a ball of fire, a lurid scene of leaping flame and heavy black smoke. As the fire neared the Tower where gunpowder was stored, Cissy saw all the houses in Tower Street explode. Soldiers must have been given orders to blow them up, she thought, to stop the fire's spread. Every so often through the smoke she could see the spires of St. Paul's, but the fire soon surrounded it.

For three days she took up her nightly post upon the rooftop. On the fourth day, the fall of St. Paul's was heard by all of London as ten thousand tons of stone and melted lead plummeted down. Cissy saw the glare, saw the sky light up like comet fire. The booksellers must have lost everything.

For the first time since the fire began, Cissy wept, kneeling on the rooftop against the chimney. Ah, to think that the thoughts of people could perish, be wiped out as though they were never written! Thousands, maybe millions of books—books of one kind, with no other copies in the world. Volumes bound in sweet-smelling leather with gold clasps. Books filled with the wonder of other countries and other people.

On the fifth day, only the chimneys of London stood. Ash still drifted over to London Bridge and right into The Black Pot. Master Clarence Johnson was there, having lost all he possessed. "One hundred thousand homeless, many fleeing to the suburbs and other towns," he told them. "I heard that more than thirteen thousand houses burned. London is gone."

"Go home to Bedford," Cissy said to Nellie. "Clarence, do you take her, and Tom also. Your pa will more than welcome you, Nellie dear. The Bridge is ruined. There will be no more diners seeking out The Black Pot."

"Come with us," Nellie pleaded.

"I'm going back—but I must go alone. And first I want to look for Bookseller's Row, or where it once was."

"You have friends?" Clarence asked, and she let him think so. "Nellie," he went on, "will you have me? We can begin all over again in the country someday with mayhap our own bakery."

Nellie hung her head, but she didn't object when Clarence put his arm around her waist. Clarence reached out for young Tom. "You're part of the family too," he said.

"I'm going right away, before I lose my courage," Cissy said. "No, you can't go with me! Please, I must go alone. I will join with a refugee family and be safe. I must write a letter to Pa. And I must give up my dowry money."

She tied her Bible and two books in a kerchief and left London Bridge in much the same way she had arrived. The ashes were still warm and the air filled with smoke as she trudged up Fish Hill. Because the fire had destroyed landmarks and street names, she could only ask, "Which way to St. Paul's that was?"

After two hours, during which she stopped twice to beg a drink of water, Cissy reached the ruins of St. Paul. The London she passed through was a blackened, burned-out shell, still smoking in places. Paternoster Row no longer existed, nor the booksellers. Inside the ruins of the church, she saw Master Francis Smith sifting through heaps of charred books and papers. He was astonished to see her.

"My friend who lost books worth five thousand pounds died of shock," he said with melancholy. "All told, I estimate books worth two hundred thousand pounds are gone up in smoke, never to be replaced. My Elephant and Castle shop is gone too."

Cissy was conscious of her worn-out shoes, her torn clothing, her sooty hands and face. "Did you save any of Master Bunyan's books?"

"Only one copy of *Grace Abounding.* Thousands of his other books were destroyed."

"Will you give it to me? I have never read it. And I have need of much grace right now."

Master Smith was annoyed, and he didn't try to hide it. "Do you understand that this is the one copy saved, the only one? It will be priceless someday, for it was the first edition."

"I have nothing to give you for it," Cissy said. "I only want to read it, and then I could return it to Master Bunyan, for I am going back to Bedford." She told him why.

Master Smith took the book out from his waistcoat. "Read it and then give it to Master Bunyan with my regards. And God go with you, Mistress, for you are a brave soul."

Cissy waited in the long line of people fleeing through the city gates into the countryside. Once outside the ruined city, she followed along with a family of fourteen, not asking anything of them.

Cissy walked until she thought her feet would break under her. Finally they all stopped to rest by a hedge. She saw a man on horseback headed toward London suddenly veer to the side of the road. He slowed down and stared at her. His clothes were rumpled and soiled as though he hadn't known a change of garments or a wash for many a day.

The brim of his hat shaded his face. He dismounted stiffly and approached Cissy, leading his tired horse. His chin was bristly with whiskers, but something about the angle caught her eye. His face was so dirty she couldn't tell. . . . But the cleft in the chin—!

It was Gil.

Dropping her bundle, she ran to him and locked her hands behind his neck. "I knew you'd find me! I believed it all the time! Where are you going? Oh, I don't care; take me with you!"

She hung her weight on his neck, almost tipping him over. He stepped sideways, startling the horse, which reared and nearly crushed them both.

"Oh, Cissy! God brought you to this road for this very minute, for I almost passed by. My darling girl, you look like a nightmare. Oh, I don't mean that, Cissy, but you are so thin and your eyes are hollow and you are covered with soot!"

He hugged her with his one free arm, and she could feel his own exhaustion. "I knew I'd find you among the refugees," he said wearily. "Cissy, the fire didn't touch you—?"

"No, no. I'm all right now."

"Have you heard ought of Nellie Farrell? Her mother is sick with worry and her pa wanted to ride with me, but I forbade him. He's too old. I promised to find you both."

"She's safe with a friend. Don't talk now, Gil. Help me mount!" Cissy dropped her arms from his neck and held them out to him.

He embraced her again. "Not yet, my darling, it cannot be. Go on to Bedford and stay with Betsy Bunyan. I will fetch you in a week or so. I have received a full pardon, as Master Johnson told you. I have pledged myself to work to rebuild London. Thousands of refugees are in confusion and choking the roads. There is no longer law or decency. We must bring people back into housing as quickly as possible. I am needed in London, Cissy."

"No!" She cried louder and gripped him again around the neck. "We be parted enough! I cannot bear it again! Gil—Gil! Let me come with you!"

"Go on to Bedford. I will come to you within a fortnight, my word on it."

He led her back to the shelter of the hedge and the friendly family. Then he mounted, swung his horse around, and was gone, riding down the road against the traffic spilling out of London.

Dusk fell, and the family of fourteen decided to go no further; they would spend the night by the hedge since there was a clear stream just beyond. Far behind them, the smouldering City sent up its smoke and ash.

Bits and specks of paper fluttered down over Cissy; portions of pages from books still burning, she thought. A woman offered her some bread and she took it, thanking her. The moon was light enough so that she could see to read. She sat alone with her Bible, her back against a stone wall, sleeping cattle nearby. Her head ached and her feet were blistered, sending pain all through her body.

"Oh, my compassionate Lord," she prayed, "comfort me now, or I shall die. Give me a verse, I pray, a verse just for me, or I cannot bear this separation, even though he say it be for one fortnight only."

She and Nellie had been reading in her Bible from the book of Titus before the fire, so it was natural, she felt, to continue on to Philemon. She had read it once before, the story of a runaway lawbreaker who needs must go back and confess. Her story, yes, but would there be a word of comfort regarding Gil?

"Lord, do You speak from Your heart to mine," she prayed again. "Lord Jesus, comfort me or I cannot bear it."

She read on and stopped at verse fifteen and knew she had found the word of comfort: *Perhaps he therefore departed for a season, that thou shouldest receive him for ever.*

Bedford Jail

The long journey over, Cissy limped into Bedford along with many who had been let out of jails because of the fire—gypsies, ruffians, and other criminals. She found that Bedford Jail now held only eight prisoners. Master Bunyan was not among them.

Master Barnhouse, the new jailer, didn't offer a greeting. He looked pinched around the mouth and very tired. Cissy knew he considered her just another refugee to feed. Grudgingly he gave her the loan of a quill pen and a half sheet of paper. He agreed that she could stay in her little room for a while.

"What of Master Bunyan, he that preached?" she asked.

"Master Bunyan be out of here and home. He has his comforts now and a warm fire on the hearth. 'Most as good as this place," he added.

"Are you certain of that?" Cissy was glad for Master Bunyan. "Why was he released?"

"All the menfolk are needed to help with the refugees, to build them shacks before winter comes. Sometimes the prisoners don't get fed; I am that busy. Mayhap you wouldn't be above helping us here?"

"Yes, I'll help. I can cook and bake, and I know gardening. Now I must write a letter to my father, Master Barnhouse. Do you know where he is? Will he ever come back to Bedford Jail?"

"As a prisoner, perhaps. Is the letter of importance?"

"Yes, of great importance. I will leave it with you, and do you keep it safe."

After washing the filth of London from her, Cissy slept for hours, then ate a hearty lamb stew. She felt much better. She sat down on her bed, leaned the writing paper on her Bible, and began.

Dear Pa,

She stopped. Never in her life had she thought him dear. She realized that he was dear to God. Shouldn't she love whom God loved? The lostness of her father was a hurt to her. Suddenly she could pity him; she could forgive him. He'd lost a young wife and had loved her so much he could never fix his thoughts on marriage to anyone else.

Cissy began to write. She told him everything that had happened to her since she ran away. She especially told him the details of her conversion to Christ and how He had not left her alone during the horrors of the plague and the fire.

And dear Pa, if I had been a believer when I lived at home, I might have been a better daughter to you. Had I been like a true coin, I might have pointed the way to the Savior. I can only pray now that you will repent of your deeds, as I have. God will surely receive you for Jesus' sake.

And Harold, you are dear to me as a brother, though we scarce knew each other. I wish you well, and that you will also come to know the Lord.

164

Pa, I will soon be married to my true love. I will not give his name at this time, lest I grieve you, for I remember how you favored Paul Cobb.

She stopped to think carefully over what would be her closing lines. Could she write it and feel honest? She could.

Pa, if you ever want to come home, I mean if you be allowed to return and be safe in England, please come to see me. If I be not in Bedford, I will send word to the new jailer or Master Bunyan.

Love in Christ,

from your daughter, Cissy

She sealed the letter and gave it to Master Barnhouse to put in his desk drawer. The next morning she took a hand shovel and walked down to the lilac bush, where she knelt to dig. The shovel clinked on metal and she lifted out the Paris box with the stolen money. The coins were still bright as though newly minted.

They belong to Bedford to help with the refugee problem, she thought. I can just leave them in the town hall, on the mayor's desk, in the metal box. I need not explain or even speak to anyone.

She chose the noon hour when the mayor would dine at Swan Inn. Wearing a clean dress, with her hair pinned up under a flowered cap, she simply walked into the office and placed the box of coins on the desk. Not a soul was about. Back in her room, she felt that at last the weight on her heart was lifted. She could almost think of her father with affection. She had kept none of the money. She had naught else to do but wait for Gil to come for her.

Two evenings later she answered a knock at the door of Bedford Jail. Opening it, she saw a stranger; behind him, against the sky the smoke of London still hung.

"Mistress Cecelia Nidd?" asked the new Clerk of the Peace, showing a name card and a fancy seal as his credentials.

"I'm Cecelia Nidd," she answered eagerly, expecting news of Gil.

"Ahh . . ." The man faltered a little. "You're younger than I thought—that is, are you Cissy Nidd who once lived here?"

"I am."

He cleared his throat with a loud hacking sound and fixed his eyes on a spot of the door just above her head. "Um, Mistress Nidd, I have here a warrant for your arrest. Indeed, I *am* sorry, truly, Mistress, but there 'tis."

"Arrest? Of what am I accused?"

She took the warrant and answered her own question by reading it aloud. *"For counterfeiting and passing false coin. For rebellion against God's Church and attending forbidden Dissenter meetings."*

A handwritten note accompanied the warrant. Paul Cobb's writing—she'd know it anywhere—with the bold scrawl and heavy crossing of the *t*'s.

Mistress Nidd, soon-to-be-Prisoner Nidd: Did you think I would not recognize the gilt box with its Paris stamp? The box of sweets I bought you at the fair on St. Bartholomew's Day? Or did you do it knowingly? As mayor of Bedford, my duty is to expose you and so I have. You will be tried lawfully and sentenced. My wife and I sincerely trust the punishment will have a wholesome effect on your bad character.

Master Barnhouse, the jailer, knew his duty. Cissy was locked into a cell scarcely five feet square, with straw for a bed and only her shawl for a covering. The next afternoon she stood trial before the judge in the town hall.

"Let her head be shorn," he said, "since she has wrought great mischief against the king. For passing false coin she will lose her family name and any inheritance of her family. For rebellion against God's church, she is to be whipped in public."

The sentence was severe and "without benefit of clergy." Neither Anglican clergyman nor Dissenting pastor was permitted to speak words of encouragement to her.

He is being overly harsh, Cissy thought. Poor man, he is quite beside himself. So many refugees from the London fire tramp into Bedford each day, demanding food and shelter. So much crime—and not near enough constables.

The judge hurried through the hearing. Cissy had nothing to say in her defense, except to admit her sorrow for taking part in the counterfeiting. She was returned to jail, and her books were taken from her.

I can do without the poetry, she thought, but, oh, to have the Holy Bible taken! Much of it is in my heart, though, written there forever, and I can still remember it and speak it aloud.

That Sunday morning she heard the sweet chime of bells from St. Paul's, calling the faithful Christians to come and worship in the small church.

I am condemned by the Christian church, she thought in perplexity. Condemned by a government and people who say they worship my God and believe the same Scriptures. How can it be? Gil, are you coming for me soon? Where are you, my love?

For two weeks, she was allowed neither visitors nor comforts. In contrast to the noise of London Bridge and all the traffic of life on the Thames, her cell over the River Ouse was dreadfully quiet. So quiet that her ears rang with the quietness. Often she coughed aloud or hummed to make some sound.

Once a day Goody Pratt was allowed to bring her food in a bowl, as Goody now worked for the jail as a free woman. Sometimes it was soup over bread, sometimes just boiled cabbage. Food was scarce because of all the refugees.

"I never forgot how you gave me bread, Cissy dear, and I'll always bring you half my supper, for you get little enough," whispered Goody. "I'm a good woman, ain't I?"

"The very best of women," Cissy assured her.

The dampness of the cell made her coughs worse, and soon she was ill with fever. On a dreary, mizzling day with grey skies, Cissy heard a cart clatter over the bridge and stop by the front door of the jail. Many carts clattered by, and they all stopped to pay the toll, but this time Cissy's breath quickened in her throat. Was it Gil? No, he would come by horseback.

The cart hadn't stopped by the toll gate; it had pulled right up to the door. She heard her name, heard the new jailer reply, "The prisoner is inside. You may go in and fetch her."

In the next moment, the cell door was unlocked, but it was Goody Pratt. She thrust a slip of paper into Cissy's hands. "He sent you this. Read it quick and don't let the man see."

Goody relocked the door and scurried away.

Cissy unfolded the note.

> *"He was wounded for our transgressions,*
> *he was bruised for our iniquities:*
> *the chastisement of our peace was upon him;*
> *and with his stripes we are healed."*
>
> *Cissy, you will know an awful physical hurt, but you will never know what our Lord suffered, for you have been saved from that.*
>
> *Be strong in the Lord. You are no longer false coin with a weak center. You are God's true coin. Let Him shine in you, yea, even in this trial.*
>
> *—J.B.*

So he knew of her wrongdoing! And still he was kind. Yet—to be publicly whipped! To be exhibited as an ugly bald wench, with her dress dirty and torn! She crumpled the note and thrust it deep inside her pocket. What would she do after the whipping? Where would she go? Who would take her in?

And Gil—Gil, where are you?

She rode in the cart down the streets she had played in as a child, past her grammar school, past the lace school. A backward look over her shoulder showed her Bedford Jail, a gloomy mound of stone over a river where she had nearly thrown her life away in unbelief.

The cart pulled up to the Public Square, and Cissy saw the whipping post and a man in black standing on the platform with a whip in his hands. Behind him was the Clerk of the Peace. The mayor, Paul Cobb, was not to be seen.

The crowd was silent. There were not the usual taunts and throwing of garbage, the making game of the prisoner. But all of Bedford had turned out to see her whipped.

The Clerk of the Peace, fearing a demonstration, had ordered soldiers stationed at intervals along the square. Cissy was led from the cart to the whipping post. She looked neither to the right nor to the left, for she was past caring what people thought. She dreaded seeing pity in the face of any neighbor who could stand there and still not protest.

"Jesus, give me grace now, to bear the pain," she whispered. "There is a limit set—dear Lord, You have promised—that I may be able to bear it."

"Cecelia Nidd, are you guilty of the crimes against the Government and against the Established Church, as named in the indictment?" The Clerk of the Peace read out the accusation.

"I am guilty of no crime against God's true church," she said faintly, not looking up. "I am sorry for the crimes of my family, and that I passed false coin."

She was led up the steps to the platform, and now she looked at the man with the whip. He could not face her; he'd known her as a child. "I'll strike lightly, poor girl," he stammered.

Cissy held out her wrists to be tied to the post, swayed a little and closed her eyes. The constable in charge of the whipping shouted an order.

At first she wanted to weep, such was her shame, but she bit her lip and thought of Christ. Oh, my Lord Jesus, be close to me now, for Thou art everything to me. If I die under the beating, I will be with You in paradise. And if I live . . . I live for You.

A nearby church bell began to ring the hour. Then a slash of pain cut down her back, as though a giant knife halved her body in two. Throwing back her head, Cissy screamed and pulled on her knotted wrists. She hid her face in the crook of her arm, sobbing. She waited for the next lash.

All of a sudden there was a murmur of voices and loud protests. A man was fighting his way through the crowd toward the platform.

"Seize him!" cried the constable, and the stranger was restrained by two loyal but confused citizens. "Hold that man and take him to Bedford Jail! He is the highwayman Gil Turpin!"

"Gil . . ." Cissy murmured his name, but she could not open her eyes for pain.

"I give my life for her release!" she heard him shout. "I am pardoned and a free man! You cannot hold me! Turn her loose or I will have the king's law upon you!"

"I heard of no pardon for Gil Turpin," the constable growled; but he hesitated, uncertain.

Then Cissy realized that another voice was speaking, the same beloved voice that had called her back from death in the River Ouse, years before. ". . . and she was but a child when it happened, and under evil influence to boot! Is this Christian law, in a Christian land, to put a harsh man's punishment on the back of a girl not yet of age?"

Master Bunyan! And here were Betsy's arms around her waist, her face close to her own. A knife cutting the ropes. Cissy fell half-fainting into the arms of Betsy and Goody Pratt.

"And you, constable," thundered the preacher's voice. "I mind me of the bribes you took in the Withering case, of your arrest one time for drunkenness on the Sabbath, with no charges ever pressed!

"And you, Clerk of the Peace! Of secret sins I have much to say!"

"Stop!" cried the constable, stepping forward. "I will hear you in the judge's private rooms."

"You will hear me now, sir, or I will preach the loudest sermon on mercy and forgiveness your ears have ever heard!"

"Mistress Nidd has been punished enough," the constable hastily amended. "Mayor Cobb left the decision to me. She may be put into the custody of you and your wife, Master Bunyan, if you so desire."

"And Gil Turpin," pressed Master Bunyan. "He who came to me for counsel long ago, repenting of his misdeeds and seeking to make amends? He who has vast building ideas in his head and strong arms to assist in the reconstruction of London town—what of him? The notice of his full pardon by the king is posted in all the outlying towns around London. What of him?"

"Bedford Jail, for now, until I inquire more about the matter," said the constable. "You understand, I must be sure. Now, do you encourage the crowd to go, else I fear mischief."

Cissy pulled Betsy's cloak completely around her and stumbled between the two women toward the Bunyan home. She hadn't even caught a glimpse of Gil, for she was ashamed to lift her head.

But Gil had spoken to her as clearly as though she'd heard him say, "I love you." In her fist she clutched the ruby necklace Betsy had hastily pressed into her hand. Gil had returned it to her, the very first token of his true love.

The crowd opened up a lane to let them pass. Cissy, glancing up, saw tears on the faces of the men. Many of the women wiped their eyes with kerchiefs. The closest ones called softly, "God bless you, dear; we are praying for you."

Cissy kept her shoulders hunched to ease the pain. Past the grammar school they walked, past St. Paul's church, past houses and corn fields and the fairground. The soft hum of spinning wheels and the clack of looms in the village were silenced today. Even the hoards of grimy refugees from London, sprawled by the thousands in the surrounding meadows, were silent.

"Stop a bit, Betsy, just a moment." Cissy straightened up to look back at Bedford Jail, the tollhouse gate, the bridge; and the River Ouse that had come close to being her grave.

Bedford Jail would never hold happy memories for her, but right now her heart was there—for a while. Gil was there.

Soon they would be together, and God would straighten out their lives and show them the way to walk together. She leaned against Betsy, almost forgetting her pain as the bells of St. Paul's church began to ring.

". . . to be a Pilgrim . . . to be a Pilgrim—" Who but Master Bunyan would know the tune? And who but Master Bunyan would dare to ring the bells thus on a weekday?

True coin he had always been to her. And true coin she was herself, and Gil and Betsy and Frank, all those she loved.

The bells rang on.

Publisher's Note

Cissy Nidd's story takes place during the days of John Bunyan, whose life spanned one of the most tumultuous eras of English history. When the Stuart kings and their advisers attempted to force the people into conformity with state-regulated worship, many of England's most devout men formed dissenting groups or left the country to seek freedom elsewhere. Of those who remained in England, thousands were arrested as Dissenters and thrown into jail for daring to protest the tyranny of the law. Such a man was John Bunyan, who chose to be imprisoned for the crime of preaching the Word of God.

Cissy, the daughter of a jailer who trafficked in counterfeit coins, could hope for nothing more than a life of drudgery and obedience to her father's whims. But one day John Bunyan is lodged as a prisoner at her father's jail, and she begins to learn of a God who loves her and desires her to speak to Him. As her acquaintance with Bunyan deepens into friendship, Cissy finds the courage to strike out on her own. She plunges into the bustle of seventeenth-century London, faces the Great Plague and the Great Fire, and experiences the power of Christ, who alone can change a man—or a woman—from false to true.